PRAISE

"This is a literary gut punch. It is the great Houdini book the world has been waiting for. A perfect escape."
JOHN KELLY, DETROIT FREE PRESS

"A compelling historical novel with a strong cast of characters. Highly recommended!"
THE WISHING SHELF

"A lovingly crafted mix of fact and fantasy featuring famous faces from the 1958 New York magic scene, including Houdini himself! Part reminiscence and part high adventure, this is a tale that will make you believe."
JOHN COX, WILD ABOUT HARRY BLOG

"A rewarding work of fervid and fertile imagination."
JOSEPH CALDWELL, AUTHOR OF *IN THE SHADOW OF THE BRIDGE*

"There are few authors more qualified to craft a story about Houdini than the Youngs, who quite literally grew up amidst the lore and legends surrounding the world's most famous magician."
GABE FAJURI FOUNDER OF POTTER AND POTTER AUCTIONS, AUTHOR OF *MYSTERIO'S ENCYCLOPEDIA OF MAGIC AND CONJURING*

"That rare book one will be lucky to find where the reader can look back at a beloved performer, enjoy childhood memories and nostalgia, join the characters on a journey leading to an unexpected battle and look more deeply into one's own inquisitiveness about the afterlife, spirituality and the mind's power."
CHRIS CORDANI, HOST OF BOOK SPECTRUM

"Brother and sister duo Charles and Cheryl Young have quite
successfully created a mesmerizing novel that is at once a
masterful blend of history, science, magic, philosophy, cryptography, and investigative mind stretching."
GRADY HARP, TOP 100 AMAZON HALL OF FAME REVIEWER

"The authors' real lives combined with the creative storyline
make for a one-of-a-kind read, and I would highly recommend
this book to fans of Houdini, historical fiction, and fantasy!"
FLYING BOOKS REVIEW

"A delightful piece of historical fiction, *Houdini's Last
Handcuffs* brings the magician to life as a group of kids seek to
protect Houdini's journal, in which the secrets of his magic are
kept. Inspired by real-life people, places, and objects, Charles
and Cheryl Young take the reader on an adventure through
this magical world."
LAUREN LEE, WRITER

ABOUT THE AUTHORS

Charlie Young has been active as a physician/eye surgeon, writer, artist, vice president of the music company Denton and Haskins, creator of the radio podcast series *Unheard of Jazz* and most recently writer of the historical fiction *Houdini's Last Handcuffs* which he co-authored with his sister Cheryl Young.

Houdini's Last Handcuffs is Cheryl Young's debut novel co-authored with her brother. Raised and educated in Manhattan, she earned an MBA from Columbia University. In addition to a career in finance Cheryl is also a board member of the Finch College Alumni Foundation Trust, which focuses on awarding grants to tri-state area community college women continuing on for a four-year degree. Cheryl divides time between the cosmopolitan life of Miami and rural life in Essex Connecticut.

Visit them at *musicmagicandmore.com*

HOUDINI'S

LAST

HANDCUFFS

CHARLIE & CHERYL YOUNG

www.vineleavespress.com

Cover design by Jessica Bell
Interior design by Amie McCracken

To Morris and Chesley Young,
and Walter and Litzka Gibson

FOREWORD

This isn't a book for just anyone. It is for those who have imagination or still have a part of who they were when they were children, for that is where this story, from my point of view, begins.

It wasn't difficult writing about the characters. How can it be that difficult to write about one's self, their friends, or their family? Most all of them are real anyway, or at least partially real, and were in our lives; though for a few I've changed their names and maybe modified a fact here and there. That said, much is real alright. You can count on that. So if you do continue to read on, know that you're not just entering into my imagination; you are entering a time when most of life, of everything, is still ahead of you.

PROLOGUE

AN IMPORTANT BIT OF HISTORICAL REVERSE-METAMORPHOSIS

"BE PREPARED if anything happens," Houdini whispered to his wife, Bess. She listened carefully, lying beside him in the hospital bed; her husband was in the process of dying there in Detroit's Grace Hospital.

Though some debate about the cause of his death continues to this day, he sustained an unanticipated blow to his abdomen just days before. Shortly after, Houdini developed a ruptured appendix.

Now a shadow of his former self, Houdini appeared pale and somewhat gray. As if the blow itself was not enough, a few days prior to the incident, he had nearly severed his foot breaking his left ankle while performing the Water Torture Cell.

The Chinese Water Torture Cell was a pinnacle act, a feat that usually left the audience in awe. Cramped into a glass box filled with water, hardly able to move from his position, hung upside-down by his ankles, he was supposed to escape. Due to the inherent danger, men stood alongside with axes. Should the necessity arise, they would smash the glass and prevent him from drowning—and stop fate from finally catching up with the master of escape. Others without Houdini's knowledge and skill had lost their lives while attempting similar escapes.

Though mishaps could occur, like his recent broken ankle, the padlocks that shackled his legs and fastened him to the top of the Water Torture Cell proved only minor inconveniences. His ultimate doom came from something much more worldly, possibly that blow to his abdomen, or more likely, just a coincidental burst appendix. But was it really his doom? Or was it just his beginning?

You are about to learn how masterful he really was—how he still is—and where he might be now.

Gone was the strength and vigor. Still, wasn't this the man who had so often performed feats of arduous contortion? Hadn't he hung upside down from buildings, a straightjacketed chrysalis? Wasn't he one who could be stuffed into milk cans and trunks or buried alive in a coffin only to return to earth safe and unharmed? Surely, somehow, wouldn't the coupling of his physical abilities, his mental concentration, his skill at escapism and legerdemain ... wouldn't this all give him the power to overcome such an unanticipated blow?

In the end, none of this could save him, and he died on Halloween, a Sunday, 1926.

But even on his deathbed, he was unique. He called his beloved wife Bess to his side and, meeting her red teary eyes with his own pale blue gaze, whispered with every particle of strength remaining within him, "Be prepared, if anything happens."

She couldn't imagine a life without him. They had been inseparable since their marriage thirty-two years before. Her mind drifted back to the whirlwind courtship. Harry had swept her off her feet, convincing her to marry him three weeks later. After that, it was inevitable that she join him in his act, so they became "The Houdinis." Those had been some of the happiest days of her life. Once he became "The Handcuff King," she had taken a more behind-the-scenes role. She had been so happy at the end of the year when Harry got his very own Broadway show, *Houdini*. He finally allowed her to perform with him again, doing their favorite trick together, Metamorphosis. Now there would be no more together.

"Be prepared if anything happens."

Those five words gave Bess a strange sense of comfort.

Houdini, known not only as a magician but also as an escape artist, had devoted much of his free time to debunking the mediums of his day. He considered them frauds and charlatans. If I may, let me quote from a letter he wrote to Upton Sinclair: "I do believe in the subconscious mind and its imaginative tendencies [...] I do not believe everything I hear or see, not that people are deliberately misleading, but they say what they think they see [...] You understand I am not an enemy of spiritualism. I am seeking the truth, but my years of experience in mystifying investigators allows me to look in the gloom of mystery where the great majority have to grope in the darkness." He nourished a keen interest in the supernatural and sought through this crusade to perhaps discover a kernel of truth, or a "key" to the other side; a key that would open the door to the realm of the dead, if such a key existed. If anyone could escape the Grim Reaper, it was The Great Houdini. In this same letter to Sinclair, just two years prior to his death, he wrote perhaps preternaturally about the publication of his book *A Magician Among the Spirits*. He had a "slight premonition" that if he didn't allow certain editing of the text, he might not live to see it in print!

He planned with Bess's knowledge that if anyone could, he would venture back. He would perform his greatest escape, to "shuffle off this mortal coil," then return and become in all ways immortal.

Death and resurrection were a recurrent theme in his escape acts. Had he not been, in a sense, training for the new goal he was setting for himself? Bess was to, as they had previously discussed, "be prepared if anything happens." And that is why she and devotees of her late husband held séances every year on the anniversary of his death, on Halloween. All in an attempt, for him, or for us, to reach across to the other side. All in an attempt to defeat death.

Little did anyone know that the séances were not necessary.

What no one, not even the Great Houdini, realized then was that one cannot always choose how or when or even why one might travel between the living and the dead and that chance plays a major role.

CHAPTER 1

GLEN CAIRN: THE HAUNTED CASTLE ON THE HUDSON

ALTHOUGH HOUDINI died in 1926 and my friend David and I were born in 1950, in a sense, we grew up with him. And on this night, Halloween, we were enthralled with the idea of a séance and the possibility that Houdini might return!

Time can be a funny thing, and fluid in nature. People, places, connections just somehow come together.

Looking back at what happened though, it does seem logical that our meeting with the great magician should occur. Houdini was not an unknown entity in our household or, to some extent, within our neighborhood or our great city. So, the place where we grew up played a major role.

I could be wrong, but I believe Houdini's importance to us, to David, my sister, and me, came about due to the particular mixture or witch's brew of our respective families. They had connections to things past and present and even in the future. Then, of course, there was the fact that we were kids. Our minds were still open to the possibility, or even the likely reality that there are such things as ghosts or spirits and the like. If that were not enough, our imaginations would supply whatever other ingredient was needed to make things happen. There should be a bit of that in any child of that age, shouldn't there be? Well, maybe not. But to my way of thinking, there should be.

I was eight and perhaps precocious, as were both my friend David, then nine, and my sister Cheryl, then ten. Precocious, yes, a good word to describe us I suppose, and often inseparable from one another. For the most part too, we seemed to get on well with our parents, better than most children might, perhaps, with theirs.

It was easy to believe in ghosts and in invisible worlds when growing up in a huge old apartment building on Riverside Drive in Manhattan. Built in 1910, the eerie-sounding and fading name "Glen Cairn" was inscribed in gold letters outlined in black on its gray sandstone façade. Two granite steps led up to a columned entry of carriage lights flanking great black iron doors.

Entry to Glen Cairn

Glen Cairn was our castle. With its twelve stories rising above the Hudson, it fell in line along with the dozens of other apartment houses along the drive. Together those apartments formed a line of castles creating the Manhattan Palisades looking much like a rampart mirroring New Jersey's rock palisades that rose dark above the waters of the other side of the Hudson. The Glen Cairn's cavernous two-story lobby was filled with frequent river winds whistling in through its iron doors. Stairs led up from the ground level to a pair of duplexed lobby apartments.

It was the strangest thing: we never saw anyone entering or leaving those doors. That feature added to the lobby mystique completing the haunted castle image catering to a myriad of ghosts, childhood illusions, and fears.

The year was 1958. It was a notable one for more than a dozen reasons. To name a few, Gerald Holtom completed the design for the peace symbol, Nikita Khrushchev became Premier of the Soviet Union, the ultimately doomed SS Edmund Fitzgerald was launched on the Great Lakes, Alaska was about to become a state, NASA was created, Bobby Fischer—not that much older than Cheryl—had won the US chess championship, and the hula hoop came to market.

At the same time, and more importantly to us, many things were happening in the castle on the river. The woman whom the Hollywood director and actor, writer, and radio producer Orson Welles had termed "the most exciting woman in the world" lived in the penthouse. At least, we called the roof structure a penthouse. A better description might be a "rooftop afterthought," as the original building design did not encompass a rooftop residence and what was technically a penthouse, was little more than a structure that looked like it might blow away during stormy weather or at least leak somewhat with a heavy rain. To David and me it appeared to be more of a playhouse on top of our playhouse. But the lady who resided within was definitely penthouse material.

Better known as Eartha Kitt, she lived as a damsel, sauntering through the building's halls wearing long silk robes always accented by the presence of a feather boa or boas in a rainbow of colors. In addition to her feather boas, she owned a real live boa constrictor! She was also a mistress to many cats. One was polydactyled; we were told descended from Hemingway's cats in the Florida Keys. Unfortunately, some of her feline companions did not seem to understand they lived atop of the world or understand, or fully believe in, the concept of gravity. They pranced and leaped about the Glen Cairn cornice. A leaping cat would, at times, miss its destination and leave its mortal remains in the building's courtyard, which was for them an unlucky thirteen stories below.

My family's apartment was on the eighth floor. Though no one in our family was a singer or stage performer, Father attracted a steady stream of entertainers. Beneath the cool and calm exterior of an erudite ophthalmologist, he had a maverick side to his personality which showed up in his interest in magic and magician's artifacts. You see, early on he developed an interest in, as he put it, "things magical" and everything that by rights should come with it.

My father, as a boy, slender with dark, loosely curled hair, grew up in Lawrence, Massachusetts. Magic became his passion. While a teenager, he performed a cataleptic magic act, having mastered holding his tall body rigid, his head and toes balanced on the backs of two chairs, with the black curls of his hair falling toward the floor. Houdini, present at one of his performances, was so impressed that he offered to sponsor my father's entry into the Society of American Magicians. Dad, only a teen when he performed the act, forged a strong tie with the master magician. And that was the first connection. A tie that bound and that ultimately connected people and this story where paths cross and sometimes bring them together, and then apart, only to be brought together again, much like Houdini's own Metamorphosis act had changed one form to another, confined, concealed, changed, and revealed. His other connection to Houdini was his love and study of magic as an art form. As a young lad, he began collecting "things magical," most importantly texts, then manuscripts, and ultimately incunabula. Years later, in 1955, he chose to donate the collection to the Library of Congress, as there resided Houdini's own library of magic. Houdini, too, had become a collector of precious books over his life as had his father before him. Of course, Father's magic interests went hand in hand with his contacts and friendship with magicians. Our home frequently welcomed magicians and authors of magic ... Blackstone, Cardini, Christopher, or writers like Walter Gibson, author of *The Shadow*. The stillness at night was frequently punctuated by the sound my father's fingers made hitting the keys of his Royal as he wrote portions of the books he and Walter produced together, such books as *Houdini's Fabulous Magic*. Perhaps, then, our home was a good place for Houdini to reappear.

This is what I remember about the events of that fateful night:

Understand, architects in 1910 had no use for cookie-cutter layouts. Apparently, they hated square-shaped rooms or right angles and loved the majesty of high ceilings.

Our apartment was comprised of eleven rambling rooms wrapped around a central courtyard, with several rooms connected by long corridors, corridors so long that when younger we rode our tricycles from our bedrooms to the kitchen. Thick walls muffled most noises. The master bedroom and living rooms faced the Hudson and west. The dining room, kitchen, baths, and other bedrooms faced the courtyard. Our library (a study) looked east out over the courtyard. Some rooms were oddly shaped, none were square, few possessed four right angles, and nooks, closets, and pantries appeared along the way of the connecting hallways.

Even though the main library of books had gone to Washington three years before, shelves of books remained a prominent feature of our home. Collectors never stop.

More books quickly filled any empty spaces. There were new titles on magic, memory, astrology, cryptography, and other topics, interests of my dad as well as my mother. Stored on special shelves were parchment manuscripts and incunabula.

Many years later, having visited the apartment, Umberto Eco likened it to Jorge Borges's "Library of Babel"—rooms and rooms of books seeming at first like an "infinite" number of galleries circling a "ventilation shaft." The implication was, as Eco understood, that our apartment labyrinth was a universe on its own, or at the very least, a stepping-off point to other worlds of learning and mystery.

And, as it would turn out with Houdini's return, an entry port as well.

Other features of the apartment reminded one of past inhabitants—the markings of where a safe had once been behind window curtains on a master bedroom wall. Our apartment was without a living room fireplace; previous residents having had it concealed, and over time it became a feature that appeared or disappeared depending on the whims of the resident. Smoke or an errant ember kept our parents from restoring the feature. I often wished for a hearth, as it had the allure of a cave. David's family claimed such a cave in their part of the castle, five floors down.

From eight floors up, the living room windows provided an incredible view of Riverside Park, the Hudson River, and New Jersey. Long before satellite TV, cable connections, or internet connections, people ran wires through their apartment windows to the roof for TV antennae. Long before TV, wires were run for radio antennae. And even now, much past radio's heyday, there remained a small box with screw attachments on the wall adjacent to one of our living room windows—something to attach a radio to and from there running wires to the roof to grab signals from the air. Ignored by the current adult residents, David and I found these wires useful for contacting the alien crafts we were sure hovered just outside Earth's atmosphere. We frequently attached our homemade transmitters to this connection with a rooftop aerial. Whether any aliens ever heard our transmissions remains unclear.

The living room windows were oversized double-hung panes stretching four feet across with a height of nearly eight feet. No matter where you stood in the room, from the eighth floor, it was hard to ignore a view that encompassed miles of Manhattan's shoreline combined with a reflective body of water that met the skyline of New Jersey. If the view was forgotten during the day, the evening western sky frequently caused one to stop and look out from the apartment to watch the day slip on into night, a usually fiery finish of sunlight fading into a twinkle of the lights of the New Jersey shore, Riverside Park, and headlights of cars heading north or south on the Henry Hudson Parkway.

The spectacular sky views made it easy to imagine that the radio antennae connections in the living room may well have allowed others besides David and me to conjure up images of spacecrafts. Perhaps the 1938 residents gathered around the radio while viewing the New Jersey skyline. On the night of October 30th, at 8:15, the Mercury Theatre adaptation of "War of The Worlds" was beginning. Orson Welles announced Martians crashing down on Grover's Mill, New Jersey, just across the river. No doubt Riverside Drive dwellers had their eyes searching the southern skyline of New Jersey for any glimmer of explosions and evidence of ongoing extraterrestrial landings. Many recall how this was the broadcast that made Orson famous. His radio recreation of H.G. Welles's *War of the Worlds* Martian invasion was too real—and many mistook the broadcast theater as an actually occurring news event: a Martian invasion of Earth.

If not this broadcast, then surely Welles's voice had traveled down those wires before as The Shadow.

I remember now that it was on Halloween night in 1958, twenty years after his genial Martian hoax and thirty-two years after Houdini's death, Orson Welles was returning to Glen Cairn, but not through those wires. He was returning in person wearing a black velvet cape with a red lining. With his thinning dark hair brushed back by dramatic strokes, he matched the Bram Stoker character he sought to portray for Eartha Kitt's Halloween fête. Moving out of the vast and dimly lit lobby of Glen Cairn onto the smaller vestibule area of the elevator, he came upon his old friend from his radio days, Walter Gibson, dressed as The Shadow. Walter was the creator of *The Shadow*—ghostwriting the novels and radio show for years under the pen name of Maxwell Grant. Gibson was with his wife Litzka carrying China Boy, her pet rooster, in a large carpetbag. Litzka, whose first husband was Maurice Raymond, a celebrated magician, never let China Boy out of her sight. The brilliantly crested rooster had played a role in the act she used to perform with the now-deceased Great Raymond. China Boy had as much or more importance for Litzka than many humans. China Boy was her "child."

The Gibsons were due at our home while Orson continued to make his way further upstairs to the party at Eartha Kitt's. Walter and Litzka, visiting from Maine, were to pick up my mom and dad and David's folks, Paul and Ruth, all on their way to a Houdini séance to be held at the old Houdini house on West 113th Street. They were especially hopeful tonight as it was exactly thirty-two years after Houdini's death and coincidentally it would have been his anniversary. Houdini and Bess had been married for thirty-two years.

At times, coincidences can be powerful.

Walter and Litzka greeted Orson warmly as did China Boy from within the large carpetbag Litzka used for transport. China Boy choked up a happy cackle as they stepped into the elevator and rode upward. As Walter opened the elevator door at the eighth floor, Orson's huge arm swung from behind, and his hand gripped Walter by the shoulder. Walter slowly turned around, not knowing what to expect.

"Be prepared if anything happens," Orson's cavernous voice boomed.

There was something different that Walter saw in Orson's face. Was it his eyes? He couldn't be sure but for just a moment, it appeared as if someone other than Orson was looking back at him. Those eyes were more piercing.

"Be prepared if anything happens," Orson's cavernous voice boomed again.

Was that really Orson speaking? For a moment it didn't seem so. The look on Orson's face made Walter hesitate and wonder as he let out a questioning, "Hello?"

Then Orson's lips parted and he repeated, in more of a whisper, just two words, "Be prepared ..."

Litzka paled, having a sense of foreboding, a seeming foreknowledge. She was a fervent believer in the occult.

It came as no great surprise to her then when China Boy broke the brief silence lifting his head again from the carpet bag and seemed to crow in a questioning way, "Harry." Houdini's first name.

Walter, regaining his composure, asked Orson if he was alright.

Again, the stentorian voice throttled out of Orson's throat, "Remember ... remember ... Be prepared if anything happens."

Walter said, "Sure thing, Orson," nodding but unclear about the comment. Easing back, seeming to come out of a trance, Orson then released Walter. Taking Litzka's arm Walter led her out of the elevator. Litzka mumbled, "Well, whatever is with Orson this evening. Is that just his back-from-the-crypt voice he's practicing for Halloween?"

One point stuck in Gibson's mind—was Orson aware of Houdini's last words? Still, even for Orson, Walter had never seen such a sudden change in his character, almost as if he had become momentarily possessed.

For the first ten years following Houdini's death, Bess conducted a séance on Halloween to try and reach Harry. After a decade, she grew weary and decided to close the book on her husband's return. Fortunately, though, she decided to pass the torch. She asked their good friend Walter Gibson to take over, for him to continue the séances. It was Walter who always tried to gather as many people with close knowledge of Houdini as possible on the thirty-first each year, when the séance would once again occur. This was done to increase their odds of success. Though people like my dad, Walter, and Paul were likely quite skeptical of Houdini's ability to break through or for the medium's ability to make contact, Litzka did believe. She felt the double anniversary tonight might help align spiritual forces.

The Tripp family was already at our home when the Gibsons arrived. A quick gin fizz was produced for Walter and a pink lady for Litzka. Cocktails and the cocktail shaker were welcome accompaniments to such events. China Boy, now short on small talk, was allowed out to strut about the living room. Small bowls of water and dried

corn had been left advantageously near his carpetbag just
for him. Munching and drinking his own treats he settled
into listening to the cocktail chatter.

After the usual catching-up talk and discussion of the
evening's coming event, Litzka scooped up China Boy,
placed him in his bag, and approached David and me. She
motioned for us to follow her into my father's study. This
pulled us away from the pre-séance cocktail the rest were
now enjoying. We thought she was going to let us pet China
Boy, and her shutting the door was merely to keep China
Boy in the room so he wouldn't escape and run around the
rest of the house. As such, we were surprised when she
went around and dimmed the standing torch lamps and
oriental table lights one by one before seating herself in
the single large armchair in front of the window.

It was one of those warmer October nights, and with
the window open a fairly steady breeze tossed the sheer
curtains, making them appear a bit like spirits dancing
about behind her.

"Come to me," she said.

China Boy was at her side still in his carpetbag, clucking
occasionally and sticking his head out every now and then.

The study was off-limits to us as children and being there
now was special. David and I glanced around. Although we
had of course been in here many times, the room looked even
more foreboding than usual with Litzka in the dim evening
light. Appearing to tower high above us, stacked bookcases
lined one entire wall. Precious leather and vellum-bound
tombs were encased behind protective sliding glass doors.
Shelf after shelf filled with those volumes rose toward the
ceiling, ten feet above the floor. Interspaced between some

of the shelves were dimly lit exhibition areas—spaces for the paraphernalia of the magician. Some were filled with phrenology skulls and magic wands. Others housed linking rings, brass cups, silver spheres, and even a pair of closed handcuffs. One cabinet housed a mechanical bank with a magician. Place a penny on the table in front of him and then, when activated, the magician would lower his top hat onto the penny. As his arms and hat raised, the penny would be gone.

On the study walls were a number of smaller posters of oriental wizards and fantastic-looking demons. There was also a large theatre poster to promote Houdini's water torture act. Houdini was shown hanging in an upside-down position with a giant demon hovering above him applying all his strength to impede his escape. In the poster beside Houdini, Kellar, another magician who was famous for his hypnotic stare, was levitating a sexy young blonde, bolts of lightning streaking out of his fingers. A terrifying magus manipulated her as if she were a puppet on a string. Thurston, yet another star of stage magic, had his likeness crawling with tiny red devils.

Litzka, thanks to her strange looks and gestures, could have been a poster come to life. In the clothing she wore, her arms appeared as great wings, which she raised and lowered motioning to us. "Come on now," Litzka coaxed. "Sit right here." And she pointed in front of her to the floor, gesturing a bit to her left and a bit to her right. Her eyes rested first on David.

As it often did, his mouth turned up in an impish smile while he nervously ran his hand through his unruly curly blond hair. Litzka could not suppress an urge to smile back at him, a smile with overwhelming warmth, one that immediately made you feel comfortable and safe and somehow wanting to be in her presence ... something we both felt. Extending her gaze over to me, she settled her expression into a thoughtful, more serious pose.

Still wearing our Halloween costumes, I wondered if she thought I looked dashing as Zorro. I certainly presented a sharp contrast to David's "Davy Crockett." Reluctant to leave the role of defender of the oppressed, Zorro's black cape remained on my shoulders, accentuated by my darker hair and complexion—a definitive polarity to David's paler skin and lighter-colored hair. Despite these physical dissimilarities, people often took us to be brothers as we were of equal height and slim build.

Litzka dropped her gaze and offered, "How would you like for me to read your palms?"

Inching towards her and echoing one another we both said "Sure." We took up new positions closer, each of us sitting cross-legged on the oriental carpet that covered part of the dark parquet wooden floor.

We felt particularly small sitting on the ground at her feet. I, and probably David too, had the feeling of being watched by the images pictured in the large theater posters hanging on the walls, posters I usually took for granted as part of our household's normal accouterments. Tonight, it was like I was seeing them for the first time—magicians in ominous dark or fantastic colorful costumes glared at us.

As she had for her act with The Great Raymond, Litzka, occidental in origin, continued to dress in oriental attire, often preferring either the formal court robes of the "chao pao" style or at other times a "qi fu" dragon robe. It was thus that she fit right in with the posters surrounding her.

She looked at each of us for a prolonged moment and then said, "Somehow, tonight I think this will be important. That is why I brought you in here." China Boy, emerging from his bag, clucked once as if to emphasize this point.

Litzka Gibson on stage in oriental costume.

Reaching out for our hands she held one in each of hers, our palms up. She rubbed her thumbs across our palms, seeking to better define the lines that bore our future. Helping to envelop and place us under her spell, the heavy smell of her perfume (tea rose, she once told me) was both intoxicating and spell-binding in the October evening air. I watched the lines of her face as she spoke with lips that were meticulously highlighted by the darker red lipstick of the period and a long line of kohl emphasizing an eastern appearance to her eyes. This contrasted with her almost Kabuki-like white facial makeup—a holdover from her days on stage as a performer. It was an older but kind face that spoke to us, and as I watched and listened to her, I wondered if one could read the lines of a face in the same manner that she was now reading the lines of our palms. I wanted to ask her but thought it was probably not polite. Then again, knowing Litzka later as an adult, she would have been thrilled to interpret and relate the stories that lifelines of her face could tell.

"You see these lines?" she went on, unfolding our palms with her own soft and divining hands. "That is your life line, and both of yours are doubled ... meaning both of you will benefit from positive things happening. And your heart lines BOTH end in a trident.

"See," she said, pointing to a line that ended by dividing into three, "that is a trident, and it ends on the Mount of Jupiter." She now took hold of one hand at a time and encircled the "mount" for each of us to appreciate. "That," she emphasized, by looking directly at our eyes, "means you are bound to be lucky." We were both totally mesmerized by now and listened carefully as she continued about our fate lines, head lines, and health lines. Through all of this, she smiled, but then she seemed to look more intently and with serious interest first at David's and then my palm and then momentarily at her own; an expression of amazement overcame her face.

She said, "I have never seen this before, and you BOTH have it. People with special psychic ability ..." And then she elaborated on the meaning for us as we were young: "People who sense, feel or see things that others may not ..." She left off there, her voice trailing a bit, watching us, not wanting to alarm. "I see here, on both of your palms, three signs of psychic ability. I see a Mount of the Moon here at your wrist." After a pause, again she touched our palms, saying, "And a triangle on the Mount of Saturn and a triangle on the Mount of Pluto."

Litzka, knowing her own abilities and having only two of these signs, was inwardly pensive about the strength and significance of this. She tried to contain some of her excitement at what she saw before her—two children, somehow cast together, both from families of unusual endeavors, now linked and poised to bring about ... To bring about, what? She didn't know, but she could feel—something. Presumably something good as then a small but perceptible smile spread across her face, one she wanted to share, and hence it spread from her face to David's and then to mine, putting us all at ease.

Her pause was only interrupted when Walter called to her from the other room and the spell was broken, the room seeming suddenly lighter again.

"Litzka!" We heard. China Boy clucked and raised his head again from the bag. "There you are," Walter said as he opened the door to the library. "We're getting ready to leave."

"I'm coming, Walter," Litzka responded as she scooped up China Boy in his bag.

As she reached the door she turned around, stopping briefly. Her voice grew tremolo while her eyes gazed at an invisible entity that seemed suspended mid-air and she said as if to it as much to us: "Be prepared if anything happens."

For another brief moment, David and I sat there silent, but with the spell broken, Litzka left the library in a cloud of tea rose. Clouds that had rolled in hovering over Glen Cairn's courtyard began to disperse. The room went back to being normal. Well, as normal as could be, given its various furnishings. David and I were left looking at each other, and at our palms and thinking a lot of new, yet-to-be-answered questions. Not everyone is given a glimpse of their destiny, or future.

CHAPTER 2

THE SHADOW

DAVID AND I scrambled out of the library, following Litzka to where all the adults were putting on their coats, gathering umbrellas for possible rain, and preparing to leave. I was a bit annoyed at Walter for causing the abrupt end to our palm reading, leaving us with so many questions to be answered. But my annoyance soon disappeared as Walter turned his attention toward us.

Saying, "Oh, I almost forgot," he reached under where his coat lay. Turning toward us, he said, "I brought you something as a Halloween gift."

With a flourish, he produced a box with the title "Ouija Board" on the cover. It was one of the Fuld Brothers' boards. The brothers had started the company in the early twentieth century, and that is when parlor divination took off. On the cover of the box was written: "To Charlie, Cheryl, and David—may this help you conjure up pleasant spirits." It was signed with Walter's anagrammatic intermingling of the letters W and M as well as the two Gs ... fusing the personalities of Walter Gibson with his penname and alter ego, Maxwell Grant.

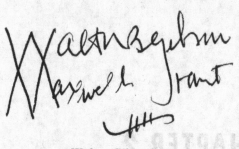

Walter Gibson's
anagrammatic signature.

In his youth, Walter had been thin with light brown hair. Now, at sixty, he was rounded about the waist and his hair had become snow white. Though outwardly he had transformed into a more grandfatherly type of figure, inwardly I felt he was a meld of the very literary characters he had brought to life—a cauldron of seething emotions and a meeting point of the tenebrous characters born from his abundant imagination. Thanks to Walter Gibson, the world had its first authentic pulp fiction superhero in 1931, The Shadow. Grant was the pen name Walter used when he wrote about the first superhero.

There had been heroes, but none before like The Shadow. This hero came with special powers and multiple twists. No longer dressed in the white of traditional heroes, instead he wore black and could appear sinister. The Shadow had to scheme, connive, and act ruthlessly to achieve his goals and most of all, think two steps ahead of his evil adversaries to achieve his goals all the while remaining smarter and cleverer than his opponents. To perform his feats of good, he relied upon a multitude of skills—tricks of the magician and of science. Importantly, he remained hidden behind an antithetical alter ego—a separate personality, that of the millionaire playboy Lamont Cranston. Still today in conversation people will repeat the catch phrase that seduced numerous radio listeners eager to have the night filled with suspense: *Who knows what evil lurks in the heart of men ...? The Shadow knows.*

I often wondered if Walter himself had a *true* separate identity. After all, could so many stories (nearly 300) purely have been a product of an incredible imagination, or could they have been built around partial truths? And what about all his fascinating dialogue between good and evil, virtue and vice. Was Walter and The Shadow a modern-day Dr. Jekyll and Mr. Hyde? Sometimes a rose is not just a rose, and a Ouija board is not just a parlor game.

Like his most famous Shadow figure, Walter did exist behind a secret identity.

The pen name he used when writing about the crime-fighting superhero not only secreted his own name, it also concealed hidden meaning. A code within a code. The nonexistent Maxwell Grant was actually a hybrid of Walter's magic interests with connections to the Shadow's abilities. Maxwell was from Maxwell Hold, a performer who used hand shadows to create the appearance of life-sized silhouettes. U.F. Grant had created a stage illusion for the great stage magician Harry Blackstone. In that illusion, there was a point where Blackstone was clearly seen with his shadow. The magic came when he walked away from his shadow, his silhouette remaining in full view for the audience. Both of these men's shadow connections, Walter felt, alluded to The Shadow's special abilities.

His Halloween evening gift to us of a Ouija board was perfect in keeping with the evening's purpose. Even though we were young, he knew we were well aware of the type of fun we would miss at the séance, given the interests and traditions of the families we were growing up in; and likely too of our frustrations at not being able to attend. No doubt he thought the board would be a good substitute for us novitiates at home. Though we knew much about the sleight of hand that comprised most magic, given our age there was still an undercurrent of potential legitimate sorcery waiting just around the corner ... and the next trick might not be a trick at all but would likely be real magic. That magic, as our families were teaching us, was actually that of science; a science that we were soon to learn was more advanced than most people had ever imagined. Either way, with the Ouija Board Walter was handing us the opportunity, in a board game, to develop our skills along with our imaginations.

"While we're at the séance, you can also try your own hands at contacting Houdini. It's simple to use." And with that he opened the box, revealing a board with the alphabet lettered across the top two rows in an arc, with the first nine numbers below and a zero. Beneath that were the words "good bye." The box also contained a wooden pointer mounted on three felt feet.

Walter explained, "All you do is put your fingers on the pointer and wait for a spirit to spell out a message. And don't forget to say goodbye after you've spoken to them, or the spirit might have trouble going home. We wouldn't want that to happen. That is unless the two of you want a new friend floating around." And then with a wink, he said, "I'd hang around here with you and see if I could introduce you to Houdini, but he may already be waiting for us at his house, so I'd better get going." And with that, the adults, along with their chatter and an occasional cluck from China Boy, left for the house on 113th Street.

CHAPTER 3

THE SEANCE

WHEN HOUDINI'S house was built it was at the still advancing edge of a building boom heading north on both Manhattan's Upper East and West Sides. Now the home was firmly within a melting pot neighborhood. In other words, it would no longer be a location where the world's premier magician and escape artist would take up residence nor be a location where notables like Sir Arthur Conan Doyle or other friends of Houdini would likely be traveling to.

Nevertheless, the aura of having once been the residence of such an illustrious figure made it a logical location to continue attempting to make contact by a séance in the tradition of spiritualism.

Modern spiritualism had its origins in the Fox family home. On the 31st of March in 1848, tapping noises could be induced in response to the snapping fingers of one of the Fox family's daughters. The noises in turn grew to become suggestive of the presence of a sentient spirit. Word spread, and soon all manner of rappings, tappings, and additional phenomenon such as lightly being touched, doors opening, objects moving, windows rattling, and candles flickering all began to be reported throughout the Upstate region. Like wildfire, modern-day spiritualism was born and became a movement as a quasi-religion where the dead as spirits could communicate with the living. Ministering to these beliefs are mediums, a priest or priestess of spiritualism. This person can facilitate the interaction and even communication between the living and the dead! Formal communication sessions led by mediums became known as séances. So, there you have it. That is how the tradition of this night had its beginnings.

I've already mentioned that Houdini had an interest in spiritualism and that he had asked Bess to attempt to contact him after his death, even though he was a skeptic. Within the last five or so years of his life, he spent a considerable amount of time and money exposing mediums for the tricks they used to dupe many into believing that communication with the spirit world was possible. It was a time when even illustrious scientists and intellectuals were being sucked into the cons that practicing mediums were pulling off.

Given the attraction spiritualism held for so many, the noted journal *Scientific American* put together a panel and prize money and Houdini was to be a part of it. The prize was offered to any person who could pass the rigorous investigations of a committee. This was to be done by demonstrating "conclusive psychic manifestations," ostensibly proving whether or not communication with the spirit world and therefore existence of a spirit world was possible. Remember, this was one hundred years ago or so.

Houdini was appointed a member of a panel of five who would make that determination. He was likely the only member trained or suitably educated to discover and demonstrate the ruses mediums were using to dupe or otherwise convince panel members that communication with the dead could occur. He was a man of "science" in this matter, while those who were supposed to be men of science had neither the training nor understanding to be able to expose the fraud that was occurring. It may seem laughable today that "scientists" or learned individuals could be so easily duped. But then, think about how time and again so many in educated societies can be led, lamb-like, by charismatic individuals to become accomplices to horrendous and horrible events.

This happens with religious leaders and politicians who do that too often. Think of Hitler in Germany in the 1930s or some of those today in our own country, even presidents, who create large groups of followers in cult-like fashion.

More than once Houdini was quoted as saying that he was not an enemy of spiritualism. It was more that he, like the *Scientific American* contest, wanted proof. Like so many others, he wanted to believe. Who wouldn't? He had become like a well-disciplined monk and better than the scientists or professorial members of the committee at rigorously disproving the happenings that so many facilitators of spiritualism came before the committee to demonstrate. And that was just it. Houdini had studied and trained in what was chicanery but also had become knowledgeable in much of science itself. He felt there might just be a "hereafter" and a way to communicate with it or those on the other side.

Aside from modern spiritualism, spiritualism in one form or another has really been around for quite some time. The early roots of the movement were with Emmanuel Swedenborg and Franz Mesmer in the 1700s. Mesmer is still given a nod today in what we call hypnosis. Even today stage magicians practice hypnosis on willing participants from their audiences. In earlier days such a state of subconsciousness induced by Mesmer in some individuals gave birth to the term "mesmerized."

But back to the séance and what was happening now ... As the group arrived at what had once been Houdini's home, Dorothy Young, Houdini's erstwhile stage assistant, greeted them at the door and led my parents, the Tripps, and the Gibsons into the main floor parlor and drawing room. The house contained thirteen rooms and the first-floor combination of rooms extended from parlor and drawing room at the front to the library and its windows overlooking a small backyard. No longer hidden by the painting that now rested at its side, a wall safe, providing a topic of conversation for part of the evening, lay open and empty above one of the fireplace mantels.

Already present was a radio host, whose show had vaulted to late-night popularity by presenting a panoply of guests claiming to have experienced the paranormal; he was setting up equipment to broadcast the séance live. His name was Long John Nebel.

After a decade of Bess Houdini's fruitless efforts to contact her husband through Halloween séances, she had handed the torch over to Walter. Having served for a time as Houdini's secretary, or amanuensis as Walter liked to describe his role under the escape artist, Walter was an appropriate choice.

Taking charge, Walter walked over to a prominent high-back armchair, which stood impressively with four ball-and-claw legs on the room-sized oriental carpet spreading across the parquet wood floor. The chair sat at one side of a large hexagonal table centered in the front parlor. He signaled for the medium, Madame Beaujois, who was a member of the Society for Psychical Research, to take the chair directly opposite.

Calling on Dorothy, Walter signaled for her to take the chair on his right and for my father to take the chair on his left. Two newspaper reporters were given the remaining seats while the Tripps, my mother, and Litzka were seated as observers stationed near the broadcasting equipment being managed by Nebel's sound engineer.

The air was filled with a palpable tension. The participants were clearly anxious to start. They had little patience left for small talk and refreshments. The time had come for the broadcast and the séance to begin. Nebel took his position at the microphone beside the sound engineer and asked for silence as the broadcast was about to start. With a nod from the sound engineer, Long John began. He announced to the airwaves and his attentive radio fans where he was tonight and what was to occur. He went on to give a brief introduction of each of those seated around the table along with a description of the Houdini home and why the night was auspicious for such a gathering. As was his bent and in keeping with the general genre of his programs, Nebel suggested the possibility that contact with Houdini might actually occur. "After all," he said, "there are many who give credence to the abilities of mediums to make contact with the departed, with those who had died. Contact with Houdini just might be possible!" Turning toward Walter, Nebel identified him as the one most likely to bring the great magician into their midst and then ended his introduction with, "I give you Walter Gibson, The Shadow."

Walter said, "Good evening, friends. So glad everyone could join us." After briefly discussing his own connections with Houdini, he turned toward Madame Beaujois and asked if the lighting in the room was appropriate for her to make contact. She gave an affirmative nod. With that, he gestured by sweeping his right hand from one side of the table towards the other and saying to her, "I shall then turn these proceedings over to you, Madame."

Madame Beaujois, making another nod toward Walter, said a brief "bien sûr," then began by asking those around the table to join hands.

Moments later she asked, "Are there any spirit friends among us tonight?" Twenty seconds of silence passed broken only by the clanking of steam in the pipes of one of the radiators. All waited, some expectant, some tense; everyone was alert. Would there be a sign? Again, she spoke: "I sense some skeptics among us. You must open your minds to the souls of the departed. You must allow all of your senses to act as receivers of a spirit's presence. Sometimes communication with the other side comes by way of sound. Open your ears." And she paused. "Sometimes by way of smell." She then breathed deeply in through her nose. "Sometimes by touch and sometimes by sight. But sight can even be with our eyes closed." And with her eyes closed, she said, "Closing one's eyes can also heighten your other senses. Let us all close our eyes," and all did.

"I am here to channel, to bring together the present with the past. Can you give us a sign?"

Facilitator or not, the room and its inhabitants remained silent for a period of seconds that became minutes. Empty minutes devoid of spirits. She continued for ten or fifteen more minutes with various ministrations coaxing the spirit world. At that point her periods of silence were punctuated or pierced solely by the blowing of the night's wind rattling the panes of the library's windows, occasionally coupled with a recurring clanking of the building's heating pipes.

Alas, for all its pomp and circumstance, once again the séance was little more than a show. Dim lights and held hands formed a circle providing nothing powerful enough to release Houdini from the shackles of death. The only invisible voice belonged to that of Long John Nebel's whispered description of the scene drifting as radio airwaves out across the city of New York. The only surprise visitor venturing into the room though came as the sudden scampering of little feet across the floor. A small rodent made its way along the baseboards. All eyes opened and turned toward the furry little creature. The odd thing about it was that, unlike most house rodents that have gray fur, this one looked distinctly albino with red eyes. Finding a crack near the fireplace mantle, it turned its head toward the group just once, showing them exceedingly long whiskers, before it finally disappeared into the wall. There was a brief discussion as to whether the mouse or rat was sent as a sign, but no one could make a connection between the appearance of the rodent and why such a creature would be the worldly representative from the spirit world. To himself, my father thought briefly that the rodent looked oddly familiar, similar to one he had seen before.

When all was said and done, the Halloween séance had once again failed in its purpose of making contact with the Handcuff King.

CHAPTER 4

ARRIVAL

OF COURSE, David and I weren't totally at home alone once the adults had left.

Mary, the Irish nanny who looked after me and Cheryl, was tidying up some of the glassware back in the kitchen. Sensing the library as the only séance appropriate room in the house, David and I agreed that we would wait until Mary retired to her quarters near the kitchen, and then we planned to sneak back into the library.

Until then we busied ourselves in my room by adding a new spur line to the American Flyer trains filling a portion of the floor. The spur line would run past a sawmill that appeared to cut planks from logs and then load them onto gondolas. A short freight train we had assembled moved about a circle track, making its chugging noise and spouting oil-smoke from its chimney.

While we played with our trains, down the hall, and in the library, bizarre and unforeseen things were happening just out of our sight and hearing.

What Litzka had sensed earlier was beginning tonight ... Ever so slowly, the library was changing itself. Though none of us were present to observe the happenings, something had been placed into motion. At first, the changes were almost imperceptible.

A theater poster of Chung Ling Soo hung in a prominent position to the side of my father's desk. The portion of the picture that was of Soo's head began to move! It tilted a bit and then his eyes moved from their piercing stare, a stare which had fixated on the eyes of the onlooker, to a look towards the various objects displayed behind a glass-enclosed bookshelf. Soo's eyes came to gaze intently on a pair of Hardeen and Houdini's handcuffs resting within one of the glass-enclosed bookshelves.

On the desk sat a heavy golden brass Empire Period clock. As the minute hand of the clock ticked forward, the closed handcuffs clicked open a notch. With the passing of another minute, another notch clicked open. Cuffs that had been closed from the time of Hardeen's death were now partially, though not fully, open, and they were further opening with each advancing minute ticking by on the clock.

These were the handcuffs my father had removed (with Elsie Hardeen's permission) from a cellar storage area that housed the last remnants of the materials Houdini had bequeathed to his brother Hardeen.

The cellar also contained portions of Hardeen's stage accouterments, as both brothers had famous careers as magicians and escape artists. When David and I had asked about those cuffs, my father related the story of how he, along with collector friend John McManus, had visited the

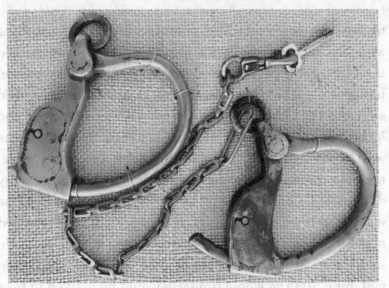

The Last Handcuffs

Hardeen house just before Elsie had moved out.[1] With both of the magicians deceased, Elsie had been in the process of selling off the remaining portions of their magic and escape paraphernalia as well as any accompanying stage apparatus. Although my dad's and John's visit had been ending and there was no reason for him to go back to the cellar, some strange intuition made him request re-entry. Dad had said he just wanted to get a final look before he left and his feet carried him down the flight of stairs back into the cellar and into the realm where intuition, not reason, guided his search. He told us later, half-jokingly, that the spirits of Houdini and his brother Hardeen might have called him back. More pensively, he'd related that he had felt hesitant to depart because of the almost supernatural spoor of the brothers that lingered. It was during that

_____

1 A reprint of Young's story, "The Last Handcuffs," can be found at the end of the book; re-printed with permission from the International Brotherhood of Magicians and sourced from *The Linking Ring*

unusual mental state he'd noted a glint from something attached to a wooden wall partition. As he approached the glint, he became aware of a somewhat dusky pair of handcuffs—of the Tower and Lyon Double Lock type, he'd said, but the linking chain differed, with smaller links and longer chain strands. Bent nails fastened the cuffs to the wall above eye level. One cuff provided an almost undetectable gimmick used for escape. For some reason, my dad knew he had to have this set for his very own. As he was about to head back upstairs from the cellar, he noticed a small pale-colored rodent sitting on the bottom step. He had the most peculiar thought that it had actually been watching him the whole time. He would have liked to take a closer look at the highly unusual albino rat but it literally disappeared before his eyes.

Thinking it must have something to do with the shadows in the poorly lit area, he told John about it afterward, jokingly saying it must have learned the trick from the great master escape artist himself. After confirming that it was okay to remove the cuffs, Father returned again to the cellar and did just that but sadly, the rodent did not make a second appearance.

He related that the circumstances of his "find" led him to keep the cuffs over the years. He had resolutely resisted any temptations to trade, sell, or otherwise give them up to other collectors for he had removed from that cellar what he described as the "last representative handcuff to be released from the Houdini-Hardeen estate" feeling he had thereby allowed it to escape oblivion.

Here now, in his library, the inevitable reason for his find was becoming clear.

As the cuffs proceeded in their slow march towards an open position, other objects continued to move in conspiring realignment. With a wind from the window, the book on the desk, Houdini's *A Magician Among The Spirits*, blew shut. One by one, certain books on shelves about the room inched forward from their positions: David Devant's *Theory of Magic*; T. Nelson Downs's *Art of Magic*; Nevil Maskelyne's first edition of the *Magic Circular*; and M. Nathan Young's *Hobby Magic*. Each object's movement was a key to advance and further unlock those cuffs. Within one notch of their open position the brass desk clock ticked and Walter Gibson's *Houdini's Escapes* moved to the edge of the shelf and then the cuffs opened, releasing their supernatural spoor, once again allowing an escape from oblivion.

Silence gripped the room. The wind at the window stilled. The clock on the desk became hushed. With the opening of the long-closed cuffs, now standing before the bookcase and looking down on the cuffs was the materialized master himself. There stood Houdini.

He had returned.

CHAPTER 5

ASSIMILATION

THE FIGURE in front of the bookcase was not ghostly at all. Houdini appeared with a younger frame, from a time when his black-brown hair was just beginning to hint at gray around his temples. He stood erect and appeared like a man, not a spirit. His clothes, though somewhat dated, were stylish and spoke of confidence.

Wearing herringbone tweed pants and waistcoat, he had on a white long-sleeve shirt finished with French cuffs emblazoned with golden cufflinks adorned with the iconic "H" and "H," cufflinks that had always been his favorites after attaining stardom. The shirt had a detachable collar sporting a small crimson *noeud papillon* or bowtie. Clothes to be proud of. The clothes covered a frame that he was equally proud of, a body possessing the musculature of an athlete with dexterity arrived at through hours upon hours, years upon years, of arduous and rigorous workouts. And practice; practice necessary to achieve the wondrous, seemingly impossible escapes that had brought him fame, ultimately making him into a legend.

Regarding the now-opened handcuffs on display, he seemed pensive, perhaps cherishing this moment in time while registering the enormity of the phenomenon of his materialization. He was also savoring the fact that, somehow, he was responsible for his reappearance, though exactly how that was remained an enigma to him. After a while, he began to move about the room, taking in the collection of materials in the library as well as getting a sense of his time and place. He stopped and opened a scrapbook, turning the pages slowly to scan articles and letters chronicling the interests of our families. There were notes from the Library of Congress and how Houdini's library was complemented by the additions of McManus and Young. There were entries on Paul Tripp and his television series, *It's Magic and Mr. I. Magination*, and letter after letter from Blackstone Sr., Gibson, and others.

Much of what he saw was merely a confirmation of knowledge that comes built into someone making such a dimensional journey. Still, information was missing. In order to fully understand the how and when and why of what was happening, he knew that some work would be involved. He had more than an inkling of what he was here to do but there was still a puzzle before him with some pieces easily in view and some not. Accomplishing the task of assembling the puzzle would require considerable skill and many participants, arranging the pieces and fitting them correctly together to finish the picture. Hopefully, there would be no missing pieces.

His inspection was interrupted as he heard the apartment doorbell rang. Still gathering a sense of where he was, along with a clearing of his mind while adjusting to his new circumstance, he thought it best to recede out of the light behind one of the decorative screens that sat about the library. From there he would take stock, consider, watch, think, and wait. He would also decide whether to keep his new mortal form or dissolve into something that felt amorphic and invisible.

CHAPTER 6
TRICK OR TREAT

MARY HEARD the bell and went to open the door. David and I also came running out. My sister had returned from her trick-or-treating. When asked, she told everyone she was costumed as an Egyptian. We thought that Cheryl looked rather exotic, somewhat of a cross between Cleopatra and Pocahontas. The blue silk dress she had borrowed from our mother was covered in colorful embroidery and beading. Fringes of strung beads hung from the short sleeves and hem, giving it a resemblance to something of a Native American form of dress. The embroidery suggested hieroglyphics. The fact that she had her hair in two long brown braids falling below her waist and sported a head-band across her forehead only added to the confusion as to which culture she was actually trying to portray. Nevertheless, she was dazzling, shapely for a girl her age, and someone who soon would evidence the higher cheek-bones of her mother, accompanied by her mother's straight and slightly pointed nose.

"Come on back and see what Walter brought us," David said.

"Did you go by Eartha's penthouse?" I asked. "She sure had a great selection of candies—and what about the costumes her friends were wearing? I wish we could dress up like them." Somehow being in the theater had benefits for these adults when times like Halloween came around. Access to wardrobe departments and makeup specialists gave many in the building an edge over what the kids would wear on their brief candy-scarfing rounds of trick or treating.

Cheryl had a lot to say about Eartha's.

"Oh, Eartha greeted me at the door and *oohe*d and *ahhe*d over my costume and then invited me to mingle with some of her guests."

"Wow, were you lucky," David said. "We only got to peek in from the doorway. What did you see?"

"Well," said Cheryl, "there were several Marilyn Monroe and Elvis look-alikes. The Marilyns were all wearing different dresses. Some sported sunglasses and others were decked out in diamonds which I guess were probably rhinestones. There was one guy decked out in full Dracula attire. He had quite a dramatic comb back of his thinning dark hair."

"Gee," I said, "I wish we had been invited inside."

Clearly still caught up in her story-telling Cheryl, rattled on, "my favorite was someone decked out in full Santa Claus garb. A little early in the season but, still, his white beard and cheerful *ho ho ho* added an extra merry feeling to the party atmosphere. There were a gazillion carved pumpkins with glowing candles everywhere. Bats and spider webs dangled from the ceiling. Everyone had a cocktail glass in their hands. It was sooo great. And the music! They were playing Fats Domino songs and Jerry Lee Lewis. She and her friends are just so with it!"

"Neat," David chimed in.

"What did Walter bring?" she finally stopped to say.

"Come on," I said, pulling something sweet out of her treat bag. "Come on back to my room and we'll swap candies. David and I have waited so that we'd all have our best chance to trade for what we like most."

Once in the room we sat on the floor and poured our candies onto the ground and began picking and choosing and making trades.

"Litztka read our palms before they left for the séance," David brought up in between candy selections.

"Let's look at yours," I added as Cheryl was simultaneously saying, "Show me how she did it."

Of course, we did not have Litzka's skill or knowledge but we did remember some of what she had said.

"She told us we had psychic ability," David went on.

I had grabbed my sister's hand and had begun searching for the three signs. "Look," I said, "here's the Mount of the Moon."

David grew closer and, peering at her hand, said, "And she has a triangle on the Mount of Saturn."

"And on the mount of Pluto," I added.

David and I held out our hands for her to examine and compare to her own and we sat for a bit and wondered about these marks and lines which we were now aware of on our skin.

And there it was. There were three of us, apparently with similar, previously unknown and untested purpose. Purpose that had, no doubt, played an integral part in initiating the events that recently transpired in the library down the hall.

"Well," Cheryl began, "I don't know what it all means. And you still haven't shown me what Walter brought."

"Neither do we," I said. "We'll ask Litzka when she comes back." Turning to the box with the Ouija board, I said, "Walter brought us a game. He explained it to us. It's a sort of séance game we can play while they have their séance at Houdini's house. David and I thought the best place to try it would be in the library. You'll see. Come on." And off we went to the library, looking briefly down the long hall to the kitchen to see if Mary was still busy with household chores and would therefore be unaware of our library intrusion.

In the library the small changes that had occurred in our absence went without our notice. Although observant of our surroundings, we were too caught up in anticipation of a new game and the thrill of a potential supernatural encounter to register the library's recent events and the now-open handcuffs.

Placing the Ouija Board box on the floor in the middle of the room the three of us all took places about the box and immediately removed the minimal contents. I opened and placed the board between us. David set the pointer out and explained the function to Cheryl. Houdini, still in the shadows behind a nearby screen, watched with amusement. He knew we would, like our adult counterparts, set about in an attempt to reach him, yet he was already here!

"How should we contact him?" David asked. "Walter didn't tell us how to contact someone specifically."

"Contact who?" Cheryl responded.

"Houdini of course," I said. "Wouldn't it be cool if we were able to make contact and Mom and Dad and everyone else didn't? I'm not sure how though."

"Maybe we should start by lighting a candle," Cheryl offered and added, "I'll get one."

While she was away David said, while looking into the box, "Maybe there are other instructions in the box or under the lid."

On the undersurface of the lid were directions.

Contents: One spirit board, One planchette. Instructions: Place planchette on board. Place finger(s) of user(s) on planchette. Ask if there are any spirits present. If there are, the planchette may move under their direction to answer questions. Below this there was a warning. *Caution: Manufacturer cannot guarantee spirits will respond. Should spirits respond, Manufacturer cannot be held responsible for spirits' actions.*

In the darkened silence of the library, that was all David and I needed to read to believe we had the real thing before us. A true device for communication with the dead. Suddenly my dad's study seemed perhaps too much the right place to be playing this game and we were both spooked a bit. Surrounded by the large theatrical posters of ghoulish demons and stage wizards, once again we felt particularly small and vulnerable. It was therefore quite a relief when Cheryl suddenly returned with candles and matches.

She sat down with us around the board and lit the candles. We showed her the instructions under the game box top which she quickly read. As we all placed our fingers on the pointer, with the wind from the courtyard window the candles flickered and let off a little smoke. Strains of other noises drifted in from outside the window. Sounds mixed with laughter and music from other people's parties from floors above and below us. The sounds were soft and would come and go with the breezy night air. The candles continued to flicker and we waited. Candlelight has a way of making objects dance and move as the flame changes with air currents. As nothing seemed to remain stationary under the flickering light's influence, it made it that much easier for us to think that we might be seeing or feeling a shadowy presence.

When the silence became too much Cheryl whispered, "Is anyone here?" This was followed by more silence. There was no movement of the planchette. There was just the stillness about us.

"Hello," I ultimately said.

No response.

"Hello, spirit," offered David. The candles continued to flicker and drip wax while we all peered about. Still, nothing happened.

"Houdini?" I tried.

A minute passed. Nothing.

"Eric?" Cheryl said. And then looking at us she said, "That's his REAL name." Still nothing.

With our increasing efforts and no response, we tried other personages. George Washington, Christopher Columbus, and others with an increasing silliness. And soon the fear or intimidation and uneasiness that David and I had felt passed.

Finally, without any success, we came to the conclusion that our efforts would be unsuccessful and we began to exclaim our disillusion with the game and the board.

It was at that time that suddenly, breaking into our silliness like a thunderbolt, a voice spoke, and it was not one of ours. It spoke filling the room with an intensity and reverberation that seemed to come from everywhere including from within our very beings!

We heard, "Real magic does not come in a box. Real magic happens. It is not up to you to summon a spirit. To escape the chains of death unforeseeable events must occur."

Frozen in that moment, only our eyes looked to see if the other had spoken or had heard those words. Though our movement had stopped, the candles continued to flicker in the intermittent breeze and now wax broke forth pouring down, rapid drips somehow making a thunderous sound as if they were the cataracts of a great waterfall. The noise was to announce a new presence. In the shadowy light of the candles, I could see that not one of us was even breathing. Just our eyes were released from our state of petrified fear. And with these we each glanced back and forth to one another, waiting, unable to even utter a word.

And then we heard, but closer this time, "And they have occurred."

"Who is there?" I finally asked.

"It is I," a booming voice said, sounding again all around us. But then, closer, quieter, and alongside of us, like the brush of a small gust of wind against our ears, we heard: "I am Houdini."

CHAPTER 7

OUR FIRST CONVERSATION

IN ECCLESIASTES, we are told, "To everything there is a season, a time for every purpose under heaven: A time to be born, and a time to die." And so it had been with Houdini. He had died and it didn't make sense that he was here.

With respect to the Bible, perhaps it was more the Book of Ruth that had led Bess to pursue the séances ... "Entreat me not to leave you, or to turn back from following after you; for wherever you go I will go ..." But then, "Where you die, I will die, and there will I be buried ..." which is the path we all take and Bess eventually took.

And yet here Houdini was again.

Even as kids, believing in ghosts—or spirits—really only goes so far. Although we might, as children, have been receptive to things that adults would have long ago forsaken, having to accept the sudden appearance of someone dead would have, in the final analysis, been far-fetched. So, for it to actually happen, we were each left with a warped sense of what was real, pushing us well beyond the boundaries of any solipsistic beliefs we might have held.

On the one hand, there was an incredible sensation—that chill of goose bumps that can pop up on your skin or a shiver that runs up and down your spine when something out of the normal occurs. Then there is a rush, blood coming to your head flushing into your cheeks and ultimately working its way down your body filling you with a not necessarily pleasant, but not unpleasant either, warmth. It makes you at once more alive and more aware. Houdini's appearance produced in us this particular heightened reality oddly because it was so far away from what should be real. There was definitely a dash of fear, but...

On the other hand, within a very short time, there was also something reassuring about his presence. Something calming, even natural that he should appear, first as a voice and then as an image, beside us. It was as if he was meant to be here and that we were already well acquainted, like old friends.

"Whoa," David said, "Are you really here?"

"Did we really summon you?" asked Cheryl.

"Oh, I'm here," a voice answered as if close to David's ear. And then, "But not from your game," coming as a loud whisper from behind Cheryl. "I've been here for some time, watching and considering," we heard, clearly spoken to all of us. Then there was a sensation, a feeling as something or somebody brushing by our sides. That caused all three of us to turn our heads toward the Japanese screen adjacent to one of the library walls.

"So, when did you get here?" I asked, turning my head.

Slowly before our eyes, as if making an entrance, the apparition of Houdini appeared and then solidified as he stepped out from behind the screen. Standing there, although not a tall man, he seemed to tower above us as we were all seated on the library floor. He was impressive. Even in the 1950s, someone dressed so articulately made a statement ... unjacketed in a waistcoat, with his French cuffed shirt adorned with a crimson bowtie. And the statement was highlighted with the sparkle of gold cufflinks, cufflinks inscribed with two Hs delineating that he was Harry Houdini, the Handcuff King.

Time had allowed him to gather his sense of presence. He responded, "It really is irrelevant that question. Time is fluid. I've learned it doesn't only run in one direction. Though to bring it into terms you may more readily understand, while physically I appeared here within your recent hours, I haven't actually ever left."

"So, why are you here now?" Cheryl asked.

His piercing blue eyes stared at us. His brow furrowed slightly. "I think ..." he continued after a pause. "The time—it is Halloween you know, the day my mortality came to an end. But I think it has more to do with who all of you are, and your parents and their friends and all of our mutual interests—and magic—and something not completed. I think there are times, as now, when— for poorly understood reasons—we are given a chance to complete something that would have been special, as long as that completion can align itself with completing something else that is, (or will be, special, perhaps even necessary, for several others—for all of you. Something out of the ordinary. In fact, when all is said and done, it becomes extraordinary. Not necessarily for the world, but for those involved ... and perhaps too the world, at least this time. A defining set of experiences where life and afterlife comingle as the continuum that they really are, and can hopefully bring about something that is good. For you see, in my case it is not an agony of my soul that has caused me to return. I am not a ghost."

"Golly," I said.

"Jeepers creepers," said David.

"Oh my goodness," exclaimed Cheryl.

"You see," he went on, his brow relaxing, "when I was here before, I captured people's imaginations. I believe I am, with your help, to do that again. Some of this is a bit fuzzy. The transference from where I was to where I am has left me with only partial recall. I do remember that in the period before my death I had been working on a new illusion. No, not an illusion, actually something truly astonishing. A set of formulas, something that by their very nature would make believers of skeptics but also skeptics of believers, bending or changing the natural laws of the universe. I know this, but for the life of me, if you'll excuse my use of the expression, I cannot recall the basics of it all, only that I believe I had resolved it. And I know by the rules I must follow on my return, rules I cannot question and do not completely understand, that I can only tell you so much. That part of this you must interpret, decipher, or unravel for yourselves, otherwise it will not happen. For you see, I am only a part of this, as we all are, just parts of the whole. Even I do not make all the rules, nor understand all the laws of the universe. As I said, I am not a ghost, I am not just a spirit."

He waited and paused, looking at us to see that he had not lost our attention. And he had not, for as you can imagine, we were listening intently to his every word! We were trying to understand, trying to take it all in, which was not an easy thing to do in our astonishment.

With a sparkle in his eyes, he then told us, "I believe I have returned so that I can make it all happen, that I can perform my best or finish something that I had started, and you are all to help me do that."

He stopped and we waited. Flicking his head from side to side he had been caught by an idea. Tossing black curls one way then the other, his eyes searched furtively about the room as if looking to be sure we were truly alone. The fall evening air streamed in through the window more briskly, bringing a bit of chill with it while Houdini paced as he thought and then continued. His speech was different now, he was speaking as someone who had to be heard; every word had meaning. He spoke with a bit of urgency in his voice and a new alert expression on his face. He had remembered a main point of why he had returned. He knew what he had to do and what needed to be revealed.

"Listen carefully to me for everything I say to you, you will need to know if this is to happen. Listen, I tell you. It is all there. The plans are safely hidden in my house," he emphasized. "And although I cannot be there, only I can unlock them. You three are key, that is clear. You must go there to retrieve them."

Before we could ask more or have him explain, we were distracted by the noise of our parents, the Gibsons, and others returning from Houdini's house. The three of us turned frantically toward the library door. None of us wanted to be caught in the room and if we didn't skedaddle out of there ... but glancing back to where Houdini had been and then about the room we saw, aside from us, it was empty. He wasn't anywhere to be seen.

Had he vanished?

"Where'd he go?" I asked, somewhat shaken.

"I don't know," David answered with a quaver to his voice.

Considering the situation, I don't believe any of us were really sure he had been there. Or for that matter, what it was we had just experienced.

"Was he really here?" I said.

"I don't know," David said again.

"I ... think ... so," Cheryl responded hesitantly, questioningly, and then added, "Let's go before they find us here." As we quickly gathered the game together fleeing the library, we began the process of coming to grips with the reality of what had transpired.

Though I don't think any of us were exactly fearful, we all were left at the least feeling apprehensive and grappling inwardly with the incredible, inexplicable event.

CHAPTER 8

MNEMONICS

THE GROUP returning from the séance now also included Long John Nebel.

Though we were already aware due to our recent experience in the library, they informed us that, as usual, their séance was unsuccessful in its stated purpose and Houdini had not appeared for them.

The three of us looked about and then at each other as conspirators, knowing that we wanted all to appear normal. Each of us was unsure as to how much we should say or even reveal about what had just occurred at home. By exchanging glances between us, it seemed we all three thought it best to keep quiet as to what had transpired in the library. Instead, we chose to listen to what had taken place for them at Houdini's.

In the living room, Cheryl approached Litzka.

"Cheryl, how good to see you. What a wonderful costume. Perhaps Walter and I should have worn costumes tonight too."

One had to wonder what Litzka would consider a costume, given the Chinese robe she was wearing and the clothing she so often chose to wear. And then she continued, "Maybe if you had been there that would have made Houdini more sympathetic toward returning for *our* séance." As Litzka said this, her emphasis on the word *our* as she looked and spoke to us made us suspicious that she knew something, something about what had occurred at home here while they were out. Cheryl, David, and I all looked at one another, none of us sure whether or not we should divulge what had transpired.

"Look, Litzka," Cheryl said, holding out her palm. "The boys tell me it's like theirs. What does it mean?"

Litzka looked down on Cheryl's hand, taking it like she had David's and mine.

Slowly she examined it, bending it and tracing parts with her index finger, smoothing and stretching areas with her thumb. Then, looking up into Cheryl's face and, sporting a bit of a smile, she responded, "Well, you're right, and I also see here you are to be Queen of the Nile." But, once again, the smile quickly left as she looked at us and I knew she was thinking about what she hadn't told David and me earlier. It was then clear she knew about what had occurred in the library while they were out, because she said, "But I think you already know what it means." She paused and, seemingly speaking to all of us, added, "Don't you?" Not so much as a question but rather as an affirmation having sensed that something had begun. Something that one, with her age and abilities, had been anticipating.

On the couch, my father was talking to the rest of the group about the hidden significance behind Houdini's house. The Houdini home had sat empty from the time it was built in 1896 until the time Harry purchased it from the builder in 1904. Why it had remained empty for so long remains a matter of speculation, but the home's address more than likely held special significance for Houdini. During his years of transition into the "Handcuff King," his various performances had utilized methods of sending coded messages between the performer and assistant, mentalism, and even 'faked' spiritualism acts. During the period of 1905, he was even working on a book dealing with the subject of codes and ciphers. Knowing that, my father and particularly my mother using her past skills as a wartime cryptographer, had put the address of Houdini's home through a mnemonic-cryptographic analysis.

Now, Father was relating to Nebel the basics of a centuries-old phonetic numeral code, one that Paul, Walter, and Litzka knew well and one that ultimately helped us find the hidden plans to Houdini's most astounding mysteries.

In this discussion my father was in his element, the academician or house professor. As the years progressed, he, Walter, and my mother would all write books on the art of memory and the codes used by memory experts helping them accomplish their astounding feats of the mind. His book collecting went from magic to memory with his memory library eventually forming the basis of the memory and mnemonics collection at the University of San Marino in Italy.

He explained, "The code is clearly one of the best memory devices as it translates numbers into words or words into numbers. Consonant sounds are used as figures and vowels are used freely to help fill in words." Then my mother continued explaining, "There are ten consonant sounds, allowing combinations of numbers one through nine. Zero is also included to complete the ten sounds. Combinations of these, with free use of vowels as needed, can produce any word, or any word can produce a number."

For you, my reader, as I imagine you are not familiar with the system, the following is how it works:

1 is the letter T

2 is the letter N

3 is the letter M

4 is the letter R

5 is the letter L

6 is a soft G or J or CH or SH or similar sounds

7 is a hard C or K

8 is the letter F or PH or V

9 is the letter P or B

0 is the letter Z or S or soft C

From this, my father explained to Nebel and now also to the rest of the group as they had also become interested, "Houdini's house address of 278 W. 113th becomes 'uncuff we tie them' or 'handcuff we tie them.' The 278 is 'uNCuFF' or 'haN(d)CuFF.' The mnemonic significance of the address thus revealed. There was little doubt in the group's minds that there could be no coincidence here in Houdini's choice of address and why he might have selected that particular house rather than any others being built. As a matter of fact, Walter added, "Houdini had a profound regard for all aspects of manipulation of memory. He and Bess incorporated the use of systems like this in their telepathy acts where key words represented numbers, and phrases could be tip-offs to tell Houdini the answers to questions audience members might put forth."

Not to be forgotten, from the floor adjacent to Litzka, a scratching could be heard. Reaching beside her, Litzka scooped up her feathered companion, China Boy, saying, "you've been such a silent observer. Did you want out from your carpetbag?"

Catching everyone's attention, "CoCoRiCo," sounded from his colorful beak as if speaking rooster French.

"Time for a little card magic," Litzka crooned in response, using her best bantam rooster voice. Then she had China Boy perform a few of his best card-finding tricks, skills he had once learned when performing with The Great Raymond.

With the evening advancing and school still a reality for the morning, David's parents concluded it was time to head downstairs. Walter and Litzka, having driven in from Maine, were staying the night with us. Nebel made his goodbyes. Handing Nebel his umbrella, my father realized he had left his own at Houdini's house. I quickly offered to go by with Cheryl and David over the weekend to retrieve it and my father said he would call the Bonanos, the current owners of the Houdini home, to alert them his children would be coming by for his umbrella. An umbrella forgotten, serendipity or fate, we now had a reason to enter Houdini's former home and find his plans.

CHAPTER 9

SOLVING A RIDDLE

FRIDAY NIGHT, I dreamed I was traveling through a forest. On each side of me, the trees sported apparitions of various magicians, not just the ones in my father's study. They were sitting high up in the branches watching me as I passed. I could hear whispered voices but couldn't make out all of their words. Catching fragments of phrases, a word here and there was clearly spoken. Occasionally I might capture a whole sentence: "Houdini ..." "He made it back ..." "... a chance we will succeed ..." "How at risk is the world?" "... evil rodent ..." or so I thought I heard. But what did it mean? A headless horseman dashed by and I cringed. On one branch sat a somewhat large raven, or perhaps it was a large rat (I'm not sure now). As I passed, the creature cocked its head in my direction, "never know, never know" came from it as if an echo quoting the raven of Poe. Flummoxed, my sister sat on a nearby branch. A bit higher up I could also see David. They too, appeared to be struggling in comprehending the snippets of verse in my Poe-like nightmare. But part of me was already aware of ... something.

Very early on Saturday, I awoke feeling alert. Like so often with dreams, the details of this one were rapidly fading while remaining strong enough to impart a sense of unease or at least caution about the immediate future. At the same time, the remarkable events that had transpired over the past week for Cheryl, David, me (and no doubt as we would discover for our parents too), meant our understanding of the world had drastically changed. Clearly, our lives could never be the same. I was brimming with a mixture of excitement augmented with a dose of trepidation and the considerable thrill of adventure. How else could one react to Houdini's return, let alone whatever his plans might bring about? "How could this be real?" "Would we see him again and if so when?" "What were we getting ourselves into?" "Should we be telling our parents?" were all questions that nagged at our minds. None of us were used to keeping secrets from our parents. But we agreed to keep this to ourselves for now. We had our marching orders and a rudimentary plan and that was all we needed to proceed.

Eager to begin the day and venture further uptown to Houdini's house, I darted from my bed to the living room window to check the weather.

People write about perfect fall days. This was one of them. Outside the morning sky appeared as something hung with a crystal-clear blue as one can only see in New York reflecting on the Hudson. Overnight rain had transformed the park grass to the greenest of greens. The trees, viewed from eight stories up, appeared as great patches of reds, oranges, yellows, and greens. Their leaves, apparently so laden down with their hues, had begun to drop off as if they were fall fruit. When caught by the wind tiny fruits scattered, creating smaller splashes of color about the park's lawns. Hearing the rustling sound of leaves prompted me to open the window and the smell of the fall air piqued my morning alertness. Across the park, the Hudson, still a tidal body at this level up the island, was flowing out towards the great piers at the tip of Manhattan. I could hardly wait to go out into the day and become a part of it. All too soon the lush colors would give way to barren branches against gray skies heralding rain, then sleet, and eventually the snows of winter.

Knowing we were preparing for an adventure was exciting. Cheryl was up early already in the kitchen having breakfast. David was eagerly waiting for us to stop at his apartment so he could join us. After breakfast, we did just that and then three of us bundled up, ready to brave the briskness of a fall day. Off we went to Houdini's.

Like many parts of the city, the Upper West Side in 1958 was a different neighborhood than it is today. That was a time when it was not the least bit unusual for kids our ages to be out on the streets on our own. Our childhood was a transitional period where milkmen and egg sellers still made rounds leaving bottles of milk and cartons of eggs at apartment doors. Though no longer commonplace, it was not unusual for horse-drawn wagons or vendor pushcarts stocked with fruit for sale to be sitting on side streets just off Broadway. Although being sent to the butcher after school for a pound of freshly ground meat might briefly seem a chore, it could become a treat. It was an excuse to stop for an egg cream at Manny's Candy Shop or a slice of Antonio's Pizza consumed secretly on your way home.

Surreptitiously scarfing down such unmentioned snacks meant you wouldn't be accused of spoiling your appetite for the stuffed peppers you knew were coming for dinner that evening ... maybe not a bad meal, but not nearly as good as pizza with egg creams.

In a few years, many of these things would disappear and urban renewal traded in the tattered and worn fabric of Amsterdam and Columbus Avenue Tenements for towering buildings promising what some believed would be a better tomorrow. For now, though, we could travel about the neighborhood that was still our neighborhood. It was as if we were our counterparts living in Upstate New York ... just small-town inhabitants traveling safe and familiar small-town streets.

On leaving Glen Cairn, rather than heading towards Broadway, the three of us decided to head north, walking up the Drive to 113th Street. There we would turn east towards number 278.

Within a block, we passed the Fireman's Memorial. Sitting as bookends, seeming Pieta-like, the sculptor Attilio Piccirilli had created haunting images right outside our door. From our approach, carved in sandstone, we could see a crestfallen mother's face, her arm embracing her young child. On the northern side of the memorial, a stronger-looking woman held a fallen firefighter, a hero. There are always stories surrounding monuments. As we passed this one David said, "See that statue of the woman? My mom told me the woman who posed for it was actually the first woman to take all of her clothes off on a movie screen."

Cheryl and I giggled and Cheryl said, "Now I'm never going to be able to walk by again without thinking of that."

"What was her name?" I asked.

"Mom said she was Audrey Munson."

I later learned that Munson was America's first supermodel.

A little further up the drive, and at the time more appealing to me, was the huge statue of Shinran Shonin within a shrine-like setting outside the Buddhist Church. The statue had survived the bombing at Hiroshima. That significance, along with its immense size, gave it an attractive, powerful aura.

Soon after, we passed the mansion that housed St. Hilda's and St. Hugh's School. The mansion was rumored to have a secret passage leading from it to the river, perhaps used by bootleggers during Prohibition. Then we approached 113th Street and the monument to the Father of Hungarian Independence, Lajos Kossuth. Because of its tableau presentation, Cheryl preferred the Kossuth Monument to the others. At the foot of the monument, the young soldier helping an old peasant seemed so life-like that she thought they might move at any moment. Our mother had taught us that the statue had been erected years ago in 1928 and that the young soldier represented the newly-founded Republic of Hungary and the old peasant represented the old government. Not being sure if David knew the history, she had us stop there and repeated it to him much as he shared the story with us of the Firemen's Monument.

At that point, we turned east.

Here, for the most part, townhouses lined the side streets off the drive. Unlike their staid East Side counterparts, these West Side houses were lavished with a multitude of details designating them architecturally as "Beaux Arts."

Arriving finally at 278 we stopped outside. For a moment I think each of us, charged with our new knowledge, considered its aspects. Houdini's house was a handsome example of many Beaux Art features. On the way there we had discussed our encounter with Houdini and what he had said. Each of us had heard or remembered different parts of his words. He indicated that he had returned to perform his best ... or finish something he had started and that we were to help. And he said, "the plans were in his house." We concluded from his remarks that the plans were in this house. Houdini had another residence for some time in California but given that we were in New York and so was he, we felt fairly confident that this was the house he spoke about. We still did not know where or exactly how to locate the plans. Perhaps, we thought, the exterior would provide us with clues.

Standing outside and regarding the home's exterior we noted many embellishments. It essentially was called a brownstone, as it was made out of a brownish-colored sandstone-like rock. There was a stairway to a covered portico which was topped by a balcony.

Towards the top of the brownstone, there were Ionic columns, some paired with an entablature of horizontal moldings and a decorative cornice. Enriched moldings lay between the first-floor windows and the balcony balustrade. Though interesting, we finally decided that although he was the first owner of the house, he had purchased the house years after its construction and therefore it would be unlikely that any of this would give us the answers we needed. With this conclusion, we climbed the stairs and rang the doorbell.

Within a minute, a housekeeper came to the door greeting us. A pleasant scent of lemon wax or perhaps furniture polish wafted through the open door. It was the smell of the gentrified middle class; that and perhaps something more, something ancient, a bit mysterious? "Old house," I thought.

The housekeeper was dressed as appropriate for this period and her position. She was in a black dress with a starched white apron front tied with a bow at her back. Her hair was done up washer-woman style. Cheryl explained who we were and that we had come for our father's umbrella. She said she had been expecting us and letting us in, she led us to the downstairs library asking us to wait there while she found where my father's umbrella had been placed. She explained that she thought it had already been stored out of the way upstairs in what had once been Houdini's study on the third floor of the house. She mumbled something about her being older now and that it might take her a few minutes for her to climb the stairs to retrieve it. Serendipitously that would give us all the time we needed to search the downstairs parlor and library. Once she was gone, we immediately started looking about the rooms. Like the outside of the home, the interior sported many turn-of-the-century period embellishments. The entry hall included an elaborate decorative spindled wood carving about the stairway. The parlor and dining area were richly paneled with a darker wainscot. The ceilings included moldings.

Ceramic tiles made up the hearth in front of the fireplace. Surrounding the firebox were spindled mantel legs on their plinths echoing the spindles in the entry hall. The mantel legs supported a carved mantel shelf which was topped by a second higher shelf, again supported by spindled mantel legs.

Of course, all of us were busy thinking. "Something here must give us a clue," I said.

"What was it he said?" David asked while continuing to think out loud and answer himself, "if only I could remember. It was—it was, 'listen carefully ... you will need to know this if this is to happen.'"

"'The plans are safely hidden in my house,'" Cheryl recited, looking around. It took her only a moment to turn and then stare at what was directly before us. "And there's the safe," she said, pointing to the opened safe in the wall positioned between the fireplace mantels. "Perhaps that is what he meant when he said the plans are 'safely' hidden. Perhaps that is part of solving his riddle."

The night before last we had heard about the safe being left open as a talking point for the séance radio broadcast—and how the participants had speculated on what secrets Houdini might have kept in there. They spoke of how odd it seemed that a master with locks and picks had such an ordinary safe in his house. David responded to Cheryl with, "He said the plans are safely hidden in my house—not the plans are hidden in the safe in my house. And anyway, look, the safe is empty."

I was about to agree when I thought about Houdini's wording: "the plans are safely hidden." Maybe he *was* saying the plans are hidden in the safe. Many of his illusions made use of trap doors, secret compartments, and special locks. Like many magicians, he used codes when speaking with assistants on stage. Could 'safely hidden' actually mean *hidden* in the safe? I re-examined the interior of the safe, pushing and pressing the interior walls and examining its inner corners for seams that might separate like a Chinese puzzle box, but there were none.

Discouraged, I started to say, "This is no use," when suddenly it occurred to me to turn my attention to a different part of the safe—the outside!

Like many turn-of-the-century safes, the exterior was decorative with scrolls that had been tooled or milled into the metal. Looking carefully at some of the pattern, I found that for several inches surrounding the combination dial one could trace a thin line within the base of the scroll-work. It dawned on me that this was the outline of another compartment. I was pretty sure there was a second safe, *outside the safe*, within the outer door of the larger safe—a place where the plans could be "safely hidden." A clever way to conceal. A magician's way of diverting attention. In magic, nothing is ever as it appears. Even Chung Ling Soo, the famous "Chinese" magician who never spoke English in public and died when his bullet trick tragically went wrong, was not actually Chinese or even oriental. Rather, he was William Ellsworth Robinson, an occidental Caucasian American of Scottish descent, who grew up in Brooklyn. Magic: the art of deception, deflection, and illusion. The real treasure here was safely in the outer door.

"Look, look at this," I cried out excitedly. "It's a door, a door to another safe."

"You're right," Cheryl said after examining it. "How do we open it?"

"I remember him saying 'although I cannot be there, only I can unlock them,'" I said to both of them.

"Well, that does it then," David responded, "he's not here."

"Exactly," I said, "but what if he was talking about the combination? Remember how my dad decoded the house address? Perhaps the second safe is opened by a continuation of the first combination—and someone has been kind enough to put in the first combination for us, leaving open the main door to the safe. Maybe the final combination has to do with his name. His name must be the last combination number. That's what he meant when he said 'although *I* cannot be there, only *I* can unlock them.'"

We all had learned the phonetic alphabet/number code and had used it between us, as children do, to keep others from understanding what we were saying. Cheryl immediately said, "Houdini would be the number twelve." David standing in front of the safe placed a hand on the combination dial and turned it back one more turn to the number twelve and then pulled. All of our eyes widened as a second door opened. Within the second safe, there was a book. Removing it we saw that it was bound in leather, tooled, and embossed with what appeared to be intricate mystical symbols. With hands nearly shaking with excitement we opened the book. Quickly thumbing through the pages, our eyes met leaves filled with handwritten notes and wondrous diagrams.

We had found what we were looking for.

CHAPTER 10
THE EIGHTH FORM

HEARING THE housekeeper as she was slowly coming downstairs, our movements were like a well-choreographed ballet. David closed the safe's outer compartment while handing the notebook to me. The housekeeper entered the room. "Here it is," she said holding the umbrella in hand.

Moving towards her and reaching for the umbrella, Cheryl immediately sought to divert her attention, saying "thank you so much." The diversion provided me the opportunity to hide what we had found ... and I slipped the notebook under my jacket, within my upper pants, tightly against the small of my back. Then, David and I also thanked her for the umbrella and we all moved towards the front door. From there we quickly left, taking the house's and Houdini's secrets with us.

Outside, the day had changed. The air was cooler, misty, and the sky darker as clouds had rolled in. Just then the dark clouds let loose their burden and the rain fell. Just as quickly, rivulets streamed down our faces and we were glad we had the umbrella to open and huddle beneath as the three of us, like thieves with treasure, scurried away from the house. We did not notice the slightly parted curtains of the second-story front bedroom window. Seeming to stand alone, a figure, spirit, or image of Houdini may have been visible as we traveled up the street heading toward home.

In his present form or forms, which he was still learning to understand himself, Houdini found he would appear at various places presumably and, at least for the moment, in case of a potential need to help the mortals advance the plan. Given the task at hand, he found this appearance came burdened by a simple memory pressing on his consciousness. Materializing as he was now in the upstairs master bedroom, he was acutely aware of Bess's absence. There had been no reciprocal incarnation for her, no replicating what had taken place regarding his own materialized form. There was a lonely side to this presence for though he had returned there were no others of his kind with whom he could communicate nor at this point did he have any recollection of where he had really been in the interim. The past was, seemingly in this case, the past as looking about the current-day bedroom he found the bedroom to be missing the bureau that had stood across from their bed, and gone with that were the personal items he had kept on the bureau's top ... his prized stage cufflinks, gold and adorned with a pair of Hs. Gone too was the small dressing mirror he used to apply his stage makeup, kohl, to highlight the eyelid just behind the lashes of his lower lids. All in all, such makeup lent his eyes an intensity to match and enhance the stage presence of the man looking out. But his presence at this moment was seemingly unnecessary. We had masterfully interpreted his instructions and riddle. This enabled us to spirit his notebook from the house. He was left alone to ponder his reappearance along with past memories coupled with the necessity of carrying out the purpose of his return.

We walked at a rapid pace with little conversation between us. High emotions can often leave one speechless. I think that is what it was ... a feeling of excitement with our hearts pounding, like something that needs to burst from within. That is how we all felt ... having found the notebook and then successfully spiriting it away. It left us exhilarated and at a loss for words. There were only smiles and an occasional laugh about our find and good fortune as we hurried back down and across town.

Our minds were only on one thing: what we would find in the notebook. On our return, the rain abruptly ceased as we altered our route to walk along the side of the Cathedral of St. John the Divine. Nearing the front, we smelled the roasting of chestnuts coming from a cart merchant at the street corner. Cheryl said, "I can't wait 'till we get home to see what is in the notebook. Let's get some chestnuts and sit here a bit and see." For fifteen cents we purchased a bag of six chestnuts, two for each of us, and then we sat on the front steps of the Cathedral. There I removed the notebook from my back and placed it on my lap. Their heads down, paying little attention to children, people climbed up and down past us on the steps while some white and a few gray pigeons loitered nearby expecting to pick up chestnut crumbs. Cheryl and David each watched the pigeons as they pealed and ate, but with the book out now, we all began to study its cover. The potential symbolic significance of the designs escaped us. We all read from the front page what Houdini had written: "*Notes on how to control and perform actual physical manipulations of matter.*" A table of contents followed on the next page:

I. Production
II. Transformation
III. Restoration
IV. Teleportation
V. Vanishing
VI. Levitation
VII. Penetration
VIII.

Leafing through there were diagrams with numbers and detailed procedural accountings. Though the beginning was written in English, much was in what appeared to be code and most was technical and elaborate. Some was written in Hebrew, other parts in Cryllic or perhaps another language of Eastern Europe. Some was even in colors. Clearly the mysteries and know-how it sought to explain were too involved to understand or fully appreciate in such a setting, a true Gordian knot, meant only for Houdini to cut through and understand. Nevertheless, it was clear to us that what we had was a formulary for the actual practices of what the uninformed would call magic; and what the informed would call an instruction manual on how to control the forces of nature. Not parlor magic. Not illusion practices.

Looking back to the contents page I said, "Section VIII is blank." Flipping to that section the pages within the book under that numeral were also void of writing.

"Not necessarily," David answered, understanding what the eighth form was to be about. "The eighth form may be complete. He—meaning Houdini—returned. From wherever he was, he returned. Perhaps the eighth form is about his ability or what it takes or is involved to be able to return. Perhaps that is also why he is here."

"Yes," Cheryl mumbled, "he did return. And maybe this is all about revealing the process that will become visible to us in his notebook with his help. Maybe that is what the eighth form is."

"By George, I think she's got it, I think she's really got it," I said in my best Professor Higgins voice.

"But where was he?" David asked. "I mean, where do you think he has been all of this time? What happens to us when we die? I haven't thought about it much and when I do I have just considered that when you're dead, you're dead."

"My thoughts too," I said.

Cheryl said to David, "Our mom has talked to us about that. We have a kind of energy. Everyone has it. And maybe that is our spirit or whatever he is. Whatever it is that we are made from. And maybe that never goes away even if you die. She tried to explain it to me once in terms that she had read about from reading some of Einstein's thoughts."

"But then what about his body?" David asked. "We saw HIM. He is here as a person."

"Maybe not," Cheryl ventured. "We haven't actually touched him. Maybe he is just a form of energy and isn't even solid!"

"Right. We should try to touch him next time we see him," David said.

Looking at each of them I said, as any child would at that point, "I dare you to touch him." Reaching my hand out and pointing my finger at a make-believe person in the air in front of me I made an electrical zapping, frying kind of sound, "*Zzzzutt*," as if that's what would happen to you if you ever did touch him or whatever he was. When I made the sound I rapidly drew my hand back as if I'd received a shock and that action caused both Cheryl and David to laugh.

Children do think about these things—life, death, where we "go" though we may not always think about them very deeply. When you are young, often immortality seems somewhat tangible while mortality seems ever more likely for those other than one's self, particularly for those who are old. When young you cannot incorporate a sense that you will ever reach that stage.

There have been times I think I questioned why the thought of death was something scary—I mean as long as it didn't hurt or anything in the process of becoming dead. Hurting is scary, but if you just died in your sleep, why should that be anything to be scared about? But I was and I still am, scared about it, that is, the thought of dying. Though if there were really nothing afterward, it is hard not to be just a little unsettled with the concept of not being at all; even if that meant that you wouldn't really know that either any longer. I think that is it: there is a palpable fear associated with not being here. But then here Houdini was, or *something* was again or maybe whatever we were dealing with had always been. Could that be it? Something timeless and forever. Something that always was and always will be. Is that what we all are? That works well with Einstein's thoughts on energy. Energy can be neither created nor destroyed.

Science can be comforting to explain our ongoing presence in one form or another. That helps me smile a bit when I drift into thinking about such things.

We sat quietly for a few more minutes; I think each of us pondered on thoughts about who or what Houdini was and what we might be after we die. Crumbling one of my chestnuts, I scattered it for the watchful pigeons. Finally, closing the book, the subject changed and we talked of the need to head home and study the book more carefully. The weather was clearing a bit and the sun began to intermittently shine brightly between the moving clouds.

However, it turned out that our trip home was to be delayed a little bit longer. Just after I returned the book to its hiding place at the small of my back the door of the church opened and a tall man with a beard approached us. His eyes twinkled behind his wire frame glasses as his arms spread wide, his large hands turned up and outward in a welcoming gesture.

"Children, please come in. I have been waiting for you." He turned around, heading into the church.

David, Cheryl, and I turned to one another in amazement, somewhat wary to accept this unexpected invitation.

Cheryl whispered, "It's a church, and you saw his white collar, so he must be the priest here. He probably hopes we are thinking of coming to a worship service. I'll bet he invites everyone he sees to come in and tells them he's been waiting for them." Oddly, it had begun to rain a bit again and the opportunity to get out of the drizzle made it even easier for us to accept his invitation. With little further hesitation, we scurried inside.

We followed in his footsteps as he led us to the back of the church and through a small doorway into a comfortable den-like office where a fire was cheerfully crackling in the hearth. On the door to the vestry, the plaque read Father McKeen. He gestured for us to take seats in the plush chairs in front of his desk. Cheryl was the first to speak.

"What did you mean when you said you had been waiting for us?"

He sat rigid and upright like a Praetorian guard, glancing from one of us to the next while the ticking of the grandfather clock against the wall grew louder, giving way to its half-hour chime. Then he began, "I think you know the answer to that yourselves. After all, that slight bulge in the back of this young man's jacket tells it all, does it not?" I tried to sink down further into my chair squirming slightly, and the priest said, "Do you know why that book is so important to Houdini, why it is so important to all of us?

"First of all though, let me introduce myself. I am Father Bruce McKeen, an old friend of Harry's. There is a lot more to this story than his return from the beyond. Yes, yes. I know about that," he continued, seeing us startle a bit as someone other than ourselves was now acknowledging what up until now might have been a fairytale. Then he asked, "Now what are your names?"

I told him mine was Charlie, and David and Cheryl offered theirs.

"Why do you think that Harry and his father moved to New York in 1887?" he went on. At first, we thought we were to answer this question but then realized it was rhetorical and just his manner of speaking as he abruptly spoke again with several additional questions we were not meant to answer. His eyes began to widen, his pupils now dilated as he spoke. There was indeed a true excitement palpable in the air as the room seemed to expand and become alive with his animation and enthusiasm.

"Harry's family actually immigrated to our country in 1878 when he was just four years old. They were from Budapesh originally"—he said using the Hungarian pronunciation of Budapest—"They had settled comfortably in Appleton, Wisconsin and yet, suddenly, in 1887 Harry and his father came here to New York and moved into a rooming house on 79th Street. The year that they moved to New York was the year that the purchase of the land for this very Cathedral to be built on took place. Now you might ask, why would this site be so significant? It wasn't the Episcopalians just trying to outdo the Catholics. Don't be misled by the fact that the Leake and Watts Orphan Asylum once stood here. Did it have anything to do with orphans? No, it did not. I'll tell you the real reason this site was chosen.

"Bedrock lies a good seventy-two feet below us here. At the time, the expense involved in laying the foundations for the cathedral was incredible. In the greater scheme of things, the time frame with respect to the completion of the cathedral was irrelevant as this was not the main purpose. After all, it is often hundreds of years before a cathedral is completed. This one is not even complete today.

"It was due to the foundation. Now why would the foundation be so important? Well, that leads me to the next part of my story. You just saw for yourselves what a

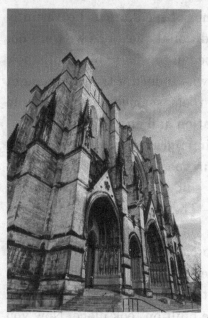

Cathedral of
St. John the Divine

short distance it was from Harry's house to the cathedral. The Inner Circle, a group your families may have mentioned to you." At which point we all looked perplexed so he said, "No? Well soon they will. Anyway, the Inner Circle had pre-selected the site. They realized there was a unique opportunity to use the area beneath the cathedral—the space between the ground floor and the pillars supporting it resting on that bedrock seventy-two feet below. It would create a vast, safe, underground repository—a library or archive for the knowledge special members had discovered or developed over millennia. Of course, there are other locations, there is more than one repository of such knowledge. But seldom do such opportunities present themselves to establish centers like this ... and there are few locations in this country where Inner Circle members can meet, study, or plan uses for the information that their kind has come to discover, understand, or advance over time."

David interrupted Father McKeen, saying, "How come the church was involved with the Inner Circle?"

Father McKeen leaned back in his chair, scratching his beard slightly before answering.

"Well, most of these repositories are in churches, mosques, synagogues, temples, or other places of worship because historically these were the physical structures that withstood the whims of people and time.

"In such places, one would be able to come and go whenever they chose and all of their activities would be well out of the public eye. You see churches are open to all kinds of individuals, my boy, and at all hours. It doesn't matter if someone appears rich or poor, whether they're Episcopal or Jewish or for that matter practicing Islam. No one would give a second thought to the likes of anyone entering these doors, even children—or where they went once they entered or how long they stayed.

"Houdini became part of the group that selected this site, and that is why his house is so near. It was through the intervention of the Inner Circle that that house remained empty until the time had come for Houdini to realize his destiny.

"But it was also natural for churches to be integral participants. Historically, of course, that also requires individuals within the church hierarchy to be active within the Inner Circle. I am not entirely sure myself but I think an individual known as John Dee in the 1600s was appointed the Chancellorship of St Paul's Cathedral in London. He was a brilliant scholar and one of the most influential men of his time in the Inner Circle.

"Unfortunately, those 'outside of the circle' who had been expelled were able to frame him so that he was arrested and accused of attempting to kill Queen Mary Tudor with sorcery," he mused as he paused a bit and then went on ...

"The tie-in with the Church is the age-old one that you may be familiar with. After all, it is the story that Frazer popularized in his Golden Bough. First came the magic, then religion, and finally came science. This particular 'trinity' as a combination of the three is what the members of the Inner Circle have been searching for since its formation."

We could hear music beginning from the church organ and the half-hour chimed on the tall grandfather clock behind McKeen. Soon services were to begin but the priest was undeterred in finishing his story.

"What continues to amaze me though is that with all the religious and other wars throughout history and the certainty and zealousness through which various religious or other leaders have sought to dominate or obliterate beliefs or institutions of those differing than their own, that the inner circle has been so successful in securing and maintaining such repositories of knowledge. It is just dreadful to think of some that have been lost though, and sometimes more than once. Just think of the sacking of the great library in Alexandria during the time of Julius Caesar!

"Well, I am going on too much about all of this. I haven't brought you in here just for a history lesson.

"I know that you all have spoken with Litzka and are aware of your special abilities. If it were not for that, I would never dream of revealing any of this to you. However, despite your youth, you are destined for higher purposes and I know that you will be true to keeping secret any information you receive from members of the Inner Circle. I am here to be one of your teachers and will help guide you from time to time. As such things go, and that in itself is sometimes a mystery, we now know that Harry has returned, returned to deliver to us special information that he had come to understand and time is of the essence.

"In a sense, I believe we have been waiting for this moment and are prepared to move forward utilizing all of our resources."

The grandfather clock now struck 11:00 and after the eleventh chime Father McKeen finished, "I know you have to be getting home or your parents will start to worry, but why don't you come and visit with me again tomorrow afternoon, or sometime soon. For now, I know Harry has entrusted his book to you. That is good enough for me for we did not even know where to locate it or even for sure if it existed. Ultimately, I believe he meant for the book to reside here, in our great archive. But for now, I believe you are to hold onto it, although for what purpose I am not sure."

With that, he gave us each a small amulet of an unusual design.

"This is a special version of the cross of St. Brendan, Brendan the Navigator. Legend has it that it was actually St. Brendan who discovered the Americas, but of course there is no proof."

Although the amulet had a cross in its center, it was different than other historical crosses I had seen. Several lines extended from the cross, curving to enclose the cross within a circle as dolphins surrounded the cross. Though dolphins were not likely known to be mammalian at the time the cross was formulated, they were thought of as intelligent and helpful to seafarers at times of trouble or danger.

"Keep these with you at all times. They may help us know your whereabouts. They may also alert yourselves as to when one of you may be in danger."

We all gasped recognizing the design had a marked similarity to some of what we had seen embossed on the cover of Houdini's notes. To Father McKeen, Cheryl said, "Amazing, we have just seen a similar design." She reached for the notebook then, and pointed to a portion of the cover.

Father McKeen smiled, almost in a conspiratorial fashion, rose, and then walked with us toward the door. At the door, he turned and pointed ceiling ward. Glancing briefly upward he said, Even on Earth, man sometimes is needed when settling scores between God and Lucifer. You must excuse me now as I must leave you; services are about to begin."

CHAPTER 11

THE OUTER CIRCLE

WE LEFT the church and walked down Amsterdam Avenue to 99th Street before heading west. Crossing Broadway, the light changed while we were in the middle island so we decided to sit on one of the benches.

Several dark gray and black pigeons began to land around us. Cheryl held out her hand with a bit of remaining chestnut that she had found in her pocket. Some began to peck at her feet but then suddenly the few became at least twenty pigeons, and more seemed to be approaching as every second passed.

"Whoa, what is going on here?" David asked.

"This is getting scary," Cheryl exclaimed excitedly. "I think we should get out of here."

"I wish the light would change so we could finish crossing over." By this point, the pigeons were starting to aggressively nip at our fingers. One particularly fat fellow was flapping his wings and trying to settle on Cheryl's shoulder. Each time she tried to shake it off, it grabbed onto one of her braids and made another attempt. I was afraid it would attack me if I tried to hit it away so I was really relieved when the light changed and we all ran as fast as our feet could carry us. We ran all the way down the remaining blocks to home and rushed to the 99th Street door of our building. The iron door had never seemed heavier than it did then. Taking all three of us we were finally able to move it enough to allow us to enter. It snapped shut. Turning then we looked out through the glass to see if any pigeons had followed us.

There must have been at least a hundred birds gathered at the bottom of the steps and in the two planters, which were on either side of the door.

Only then did it dawn on us that we were not alone in the entryway and that a rather unremarkable-looking older man was gazing at us intently.

"You really do not have to be frightened of them," he said, letting out a hissing sound at the end of his sentence. "They were just giving me a helping hand in hurrying you along home as I was growing tired of waiting for you. *Sssss.* If you just hand over the notebook, I can be on my way and you all can go upstairs so that your parents will not have to start worrying about you. *Sssss.*"

With that, he stretched out his hand towards me and as he did so, two red flashes were visible from a most extraordinary ring on his finger. It appeared to be two snakes inter-coiled, and the red flashes were coming from the sun that was coming through the outside door, reflecting from what seemed to be rubies held in their mouths.

Taking my eyes away from the ring, I said, "What notebook are you talking about?" The book actually seemed to be radiating warmth now, like it was fusing itself to my back, becoming a very part of my skin. No matter what though, he wasn't getting the notebook and that was clear to me, as I was sure it was to David and Cheryl. "And who are you anyway?"

The stranger responded, "Who I am is of no consequence to you. You are all foolish children playing games with forces that are only meant to be used by the Outer Circle. *Sssss*. It is not just the Inner Circle that can know such things. We all became aware at the same time and know that Houdini is back, so you are merely delaying the inevitable if you do not acquiesce to my request to give me the book. *Sssss*."

Cheryl said, "no one has told us about the Outer Circle, and we certainly are not playing games."

Before he had a chance to answer, she pulled her hand from her pocket, tightly holding the amulet Father McKeen had given her.

"Somehow, I think you will let us alone. Even if we did have a book with us, we certainly are not going to just hand it over to some stranger."

I had anxiously been watching the lobby through the second door of the vestibule, the door that had been sequestering us from the main lobby. I was hoping that someone would come out so that we could make our getaway. Whether luck, timing, or something about the amulet now in Cheryl's hand, Moses, our doorman, then appeared.

He opened the door, saying, "Come on in kids, and you, sir, who was it you were coming to visit?"

The stranger gave no reply but turned and appearing to have no difficulty opening the great iron door, abruptly and quickly stepped out. Although his appearance at first glance had been unremarkable and certainly not alarming, his eyes had seemed to smolder when he had spoken of forces that we were not meant to use. With great relief, we all rushed past Moses and thanked him as we headed for the elevator. In the elevator, Cheryl happened to reach in and feel the amulet from Father McKeen she had placed into a side pocket of her skirt. It was warm. "Feel your amulets," she said. Ours were warm too. Was it an attempt to warn us of the danger that waited for us in the lobby and we had just escaped?

The stranger headed up Riverside Drive and kept going until he reached the statue of Shinran Shonin outside the Buddhist Church. Glancing over his shoulder to make sure there were no passers-by, he reached out his hand and, with a gesture, a humming vibration began enveloping the pavement he was standing on. The man appeared to vanish into thin air. He re-materialized elsewhere in a softly lit subterranean room that was already occupied with a number of distinguished-looking gentlemen and a lady or two, cocktail glasses raised to their lips and conversing in hushed tones. Cigarette smoke filled the air. How far he had traveled in place and time was not clear. Was it a trick, a passageway, an illusion like Houdini's walking through walls or vanishing a whole elephant at the Hippodrome?

The group of bodies was of astonishingly disparate shapes and sizes. In particular, a trio stood out due to their exceptionally pallid complexions. The first was an extremely short and rotund woman who bore an uncanny resemblance to a barrel topped with shaggy, very blonde hair. Not a natural blonde either, but one that had been bleached to an almost straw-like color and texture. Next to her stood a man with a rodent-like face, sported a thin mustache that resembled rat whiskers, and had very long pale hands. Seated beside the barrel-shaped lady was a strikingly tall and thin woman. She seemed much older although she still had long jet-black hair. On her wrinkled face, she wore cake makeup and had lipsticked, bright red lips. Her dress was nearly see-through.

The air was abuzz with all of the emotions as tongues wagged unceasingly with intermittent sounds of hissing, squeaks, and squeals. Milo Beard, for that was the stranger's name, stepped forward out from the dim light into which he had materialized, into the less dim light and into their midst. A hush fell as they awaited the news.

"Sssssorry to say my friends, but this will not be the simple task we had hoped for. I fear that these children may not be as innocent as we had believed. They may quite well be correct in their belief that Harry had a special purpose in choosing them to find and bring his missing writings to light at this time. *Sssss*."

The "barrel" cleared her throat and cooed, "Please Milo, come sit here by me and tell all about what you have been up to with those children." She motioned to the limpid figure with the mustache, "Please bring a chair for Milo and see if you can materialize another martini for me while you are at it. Two olives, please."

"Of course, Mother," he responded and headed across the room to an alcove, returning with both in a blink of an eye.

"Oh, Robert," the barrel cooed again, "you are so good to Mother." She moved over and patted beside her on the couch. "Please come sit with me."

Without much enthusiasm, he squeezed beside her and they all turned their attention to Milo. Milo proceeded to tell them of how he had summoned the darker pigeons to chase the children back to him but he had been too late for they had already met with Father McKeen—"*Ssss*, if it had not been for that Inner Circle aficionado I would have the book in my hands right now."

The question on everyone's mind was whether he or she could prevent the book from falling permanently into the hands of the Inner Circle. Milo's eyes focused on the dark-haired thin woman and his mouth turned up at the corners in a remarkable fashion. With this sinister smile in place he said, "Ariel, with your ability to see, what have you learned as to how Houdini returned?"

It was Ariel who had "seen" the importance of the hand-cuffs in the library at our home, cluing in the Outer Circle as to how those cuffs had somehow facilitated Houdini's presence.

The discussion then centered on the cuffs, their connection as to where Houdini had been, and how he had returned. Soon, a plan was hatched to retrieve them too.

CHAPTER 12

A BIT MORE HISTORY

THE MATERIAL that follows in *Philosophy of the Circle* is meant to give the reader an appreciation for how things in life can interconnect and how true magic is neither stage magic nor wizardry. True magic is the employment of man's understanding of the basic essence and power of nature around us along with how to control these great forces.

Philosophy of the Circle is an introduction, or primer, to the historical figures who grasped or began to know the scientific principles that underlay these forces.

Material presented in *The Inner Circle* is provided as a guide to the forces men sought to control as well as an explanation regarding the development of organizations to help promote and protect such information.

It is helpful to understand these things to appreciate exactly what it is Houdini has "discovered" and recorded in his hidden notebook. This is the material that the children now had in their possession ... powerful knowledge that those within The Inner Circle would want to protect, while others now being *The Outer Circle* would want to exploit with evil intent.

Philosophy of the Inner Circle

Things can interconnect in life. Some call it chance, while others call it coincidence. But this is not always so. It can be by design. Such is the case with true magic—being neither stage magic nor wizardry but rather the employment of man's understanding of nature and how we can interconnect with and control the great forces that are around us.

This is what Houdini had discovered, learned, and recorded in his notebook and what we as children were about to learn.

Throughout points in history, there were people who sought to control and explain and also protect such information.

Those who sought to use the knowledge as a source for good had formed a group known as *The Inner Circle*. But there were also others outside the circle with some of this knowledge who wished to exploit what they knew toward evil or self-serving ends. They formed a group known as *The Outer Circle*. Some of *The Outer Circle* were those who had been expelled from *The Inner Circle*.

Looking back at our own country's history, our first president, George Washington, was involved with *The Inner Circle*.

Understanding the power of location, he and Pierre L'Enfant, the architect and designer who was also with *The Inner Circle,* chose a location for our capital city based on celestial calculation.

Reaching further back, there were those in the 1500s who sought to somehow simultaneously explain the laws of the universe, life and death, and every day natural occurrences. Scientist or charlatan, magician or alchemist, some were more one than the other while others were all in one. Whatever their pursuit, ultimately it was toward man's control of and a search for forces that would allow him to master his own destiny alive or dead. There were strong beliefs in natural and supernatural forces. In a way, it was much like it is today but the players were all part of the same club, albeit at times some part of the Inner Circle. Few were considered on the fringe, much less lunatics, for their far-out beliefs. Today we might think their behavior odd but you must remember that they didn't know what we know today and much of what they did discover laid the foundation of modern science.

Recall that with his telescope Galileo brought planets closer, proving their existence and providing an ability to watch the heavens above. With the existence of such an instrument, it was not hard to imagine, argue, or even understand that one might need only the right tool, formula, or ritual to actually communicate with the spirit world.

Kepler as a scientist developed the laws of planetary motion, providing that planets move in elliptical rather than circular orbit about the Sun. At the same time, as an astrologer practicing pseudoscience, he was well known as a predictor of celestially influenced events.

There was much magic at work and where science left off, religion and mysticism were quick to fill in. Always there was the search for exactly how new knowledge danced with and either supported or unraveled religious belief or sacred dogma. Whether a circle or an ellipse, the mathematical purity associated with these shapes no doubt lay at the root of their earliest inclusion in magic rites. Observations from Galileo, Copernicus, or Kepler merely confirmed the natural order of the universe and that all things are connected. The circle WAS sacred. One merely had to find that key, like the philosopher's stone, wherein lead could become gold or the living could meet with the dead—the key whereby one could manipulate the universe.

As far back as one looks, magic circles have been a part of the human experience. The Etruscans (and later the Romans) would mark the boundaries of a new town with a ceremonial drawing of a circle around the territory. The rite would begin with a white bull and cow moving a plow. The plowman would move with his left or auspicious side towards the town, outlining the pomerium. The plow would be lifted where gates were proposed. At these points the magic line would be broken. At these points, purification acts had to be performed before entering.

The magic circle was sacred. It symbolized and functioned as a space where pure rites occurred. It was a place of harmony and concentrated power. A place where one could transcend the physical or practice the knowledge needed to unbridle the forces of the universe, to become one with them or to use such special powers for righteous deeds.

The magic circle was known to have four cardinal points.

The north, associated with the element of earth, was a source of great power. Never touched by the sun, it could also be associated with darkness and the unknown.

South, associated with the sun, was the element of fire and the zenith of intellect.

East, the element of air, represented our highest consciousness with the quality of enlightenment and mysticism.

West, the element of water, was associated with creativity and fertility.

Other geometric shapes were also recognized as harmonious with nature, forming building blocks so to speak, and all parts of the puzzle—such as the pentangle or pentagram. Often a symbol of witchcraft, the star form symbolized the spirit bringing the elements of earth, air, fire, and water into natural harmony with the "true spirit" at the top point. Sigillum Dei aemaeth, the Seal of the Truth of God from the thirteenth century, refined by John Dee and finalized by Athanasius Kircher, is a remarkable example of the complex shapes, geometry, and thought that went into such symbols. Again, the star, or pentagram, along with septagons, would be enclosed by the circle, the penultimate shape. The ultimate shape, being that of God, remained invisible, elusive, and, but for a few, unknown.

CHAPTER 13

THE INNER CIRCLE

TRADITIONAL MAGICIANS use illusion practices to "pretend" to accomplish all the different manipulations of physical and spiritual matter that the alchemists, physicists, physicians, mathematicians, astronomers, scientists, and theologians have sought to understand, explain, or control. It is therefore easy to understand that when looking at the various categories of illusion practices for stage magic, the "pretend" powers practiced by magicians are synonymous with the power or understandings sought by the various other groups. The categories for manipulations are held in common by all the groups and include the following:

Production: Something is produced from "thin air" so to speak—a rabbit from a hat, water in an empty glass.

Transformation: Changing one thing into another—a bird placed in a box, the box is then closed. An incantation is recited and the box reopened. In place of a bird, flowers are now within the box.

Restoration: Fixing something that is broken—a man is placed in a box and then sawed in half. The box is separated, the pieces then reunited and opened. The man steps out whole.

Teleportation: Moving one object to another location in space instantaneously—a lion is placed in a cage on one side of the stage and then covered. In a previously empty cage on the other side of the stage, the lion appears.

Vanishing: Making something disappear—a woman is placed within a mystical cabinet and the cabinet closed. A wand is waved, the cabinet reopened. The woman has disappeared.

Levitation: Defying gravity—a card rises from the deck or a child rises from a platform and floats in mid-air.

Penetration: Passing through a solid substance, leaving the substance intact—two rings are linked, one passing easily through the other when moments before they both appeared solid.

More recently, other terms have made their way into this lexicon. For example:

Materialization: Transforming from the invisible state into the visible.

Perhaps the newest term, introduced by particle physicists in the twentieth century, is quantum entanglement.

Quantum Entanglement: This is a phenomenon that Albert Einstein called "spooky action at a distance." In quantum physics, entangled particles remain connected so that actions performed on one affect the other, even when separated by great distances ... even, let's say, for instance, if one turned a particle or object on the earth, and simultaneously its entangled particle or object on the moon would turn similarly and instantaneously.

The properties causing such actions to occur had many wonderful potential applications. All looked forward to the time when the theory could be put into practice.

The difference between magical transformation or production as in stage magic or any of the categories of natural or real transformation or production or the rest, is where the groups divide. Stage magic is just illusionary practices of the showman. When these manipulations occur for real, such were the skills learned by those of the two circles.

For proof that the categories of transformation are as applicable to natural forces as they are to stage magic, one merely needs to observe the obvious in nature.

In case you find this hard to believe, some of these things have already been observed in the wonders of nature. There is the *transformation* of the caterpillar through the chrysalis to the butterfly. There is the seed turning into the tree. Water can appear on materials when it hasn't rained (*production* or condensation?). This was proof to the alchemist that one just had to delve deep enough into the science of nature to find the secrets of all categories of magic, and therein the knowledge of how to make such things happen. Even some theologians eventually came to reconcile science and the origins of life with religion. In the 1900s, the Jesuit Father Teilhard de Chardin wrote eloquently about placing a few chemicals in a bell jar and then running an electric current through it. On examination one could then find some amino acids, the building blocks of all life—*transformation, production,* evolution? Man had crawled up from and out of the primordial gruel!

Practitioners of the Ars Magica in the 1500s were frequently interested in the same skills that were being attained by those studying scientific pursuits. Some magicians even applied such skills to creating great automatons, talking heads, mannequins, all mechanical in nature, but wondrous and seemingly alive.

Seeking to spread knowledge but also wanting to be careful as to whom the knowledge reached and to what ends it might be employed, secret societies came about whereby individuals could learn and transfer skills. Members took oaths to never reveal to those outside what was learned within. Organizations of Magic Circles were formed—groups of "Magicians." These did indeed include stage magicians; in fact, all who joined professed and actually had an interest in magic. But the circles were also filled with members from all the other groups seeking the categorical knowledge of *production, transformation, restoration, teleportation, vanishing,* and *levitation.*

Careful to limit the circulation of information that accumulated regarding science-magic rather than stage magic, an "Inner Circle" of these Magic Circles developed over time. These individuals were the ones who, through intellect, came to possess at least the rudiments, if not all, of the real knowledge necessary to practice ACTUAL *production, transformation, restoration, teleportation, vanishing, and levitation* and not just magic by illusion. These men (and women too) of The Inner Circle were neither necessarily kings nor queens, nor presidents or prime ministers. These people of The Inner Circle were the true masters of the universe. They were somewhat like Stephen Vincent Benet's civilization of Babylon, they were men, just ordinary men, neither wizards nor gods. Some were, however, demons. Or at least there were men who became corrupted by such power. And when that happened, those who sought to use such power for evil, were banished from The Inner Circle. Unfortunately, the powers they had learned could not be taken back. And so there developed an ongoing struggle of greater good and greater evil. Those who could learn the secrets and remain true to the powers of good and those who, even with all their intellect, succumbed to the temptation and practiced the corruption of power for evil. Certainly, you have heard or know of some of these. Who hasn't heard of the Salem Witch Trials? Or going back further, the name Caligula may come to mind. More recently, Mengele, Mussolini, Stalin, Franco, or Hitler are names that give one pause. You probably have a few names in your own mind you could add to this list. Today we might look within the ranks of our politicians.

History is replete with those who became corrupted and lost their way. Some become incalculably evil.

CHAPTER 14

RETURN FROM THE HOME OF HOUDINI

HAVING MADE it safely into the apartment, we followed Cheryl through the hallway to her room. All of us were shaken by our experiences returning home: meeting Father McKeen, then our harrowing experience being chased by birds, and then being followed by our encounter with the evil stranger in our lobby, but the notebook beckoned! And our curiosity to learn more about its contents prevailed.

I handed the notebook to David. He placed it on Cheryl's vanity and said, "most of it is in code" as he viewed and flipped through the pages. Much of what he saw resembled the following:

$$\sum n=164n\sum n=164n$$

$$f(x) > 0\int$$

Houdini, never having even finished high school, had through the course of his life come to master more languages and science than many of those who had gone on to prestigious universities and obtained a master's or doctorate degree. His thirst for knowledge and learning was something his Rabbinical father had bestowed upon him as a legacy. Like many immigrant children of the time, he had grown up with a mother tongue different than that of his new homeland. With Hungarian, Yiddish, and Hebrew being the primary tongues heard by his ears, he became conversant in understanding and speaking a lingual stew early on.

Of course, what we thought we would find upon further reading through the pages was a set of incantations or spells. Sort of a hocus pocus with some extra touches of Salem witchcraft[2] to bring about "Houdini's Fabulous Magic." That was our age showing.

The sigma notations, function signs, and large pi signs had the look of a code or an ancient language but in reality, they were not. It took Cheryl, being a little older, to understand what the writings were really about. It was math and its cousins. The chapters contained page after page of mathematical, chemical, and physics formulas. There were also asterisks, notations, and references to correspondence with his contemporaries: the Indian and Italian physicists Satyendra Nath Bose and Enrico Fermi, along with the Germans Albert Einstein and Max Planck. Houdini's years of travels and notoriety had made it easy to develop such acquaintances. Few, outside of a select group, knew that his intelligence went far beyond that of a master showman and escape artist. There were hints at times in some of his published works that there was

---

2 N.B. The first person ever put to death in the colonies had the surname "Young" (a good witch it should be noted).

much more to this man, but it was a very small group who understood the true breadth of Houdini's mind.

In a time before cyclotrons and particle accelerators and only a growing knowledge of quarks and bosons, Houdini was working on formulas, as were the other particle physicists. As magic and science were commingled through the ages, Houdini—magician and mathematician—was understanding and codifying. Space and time are a fabric. Light is a wave and a particle. Energy and mass are interchangeable. How otherwise particles without mass can develop mass—seemingly something from nothing. Nuclear physics and the study of subatomic particles held the keys to the structure of matter as well as to the absolute power over nature. Real magic.

The material in the book was far too advanced for us to unravel or use ourselves, but we did grasp the significance of the material and why it should not slip into the wrong hands.

What had seemed like minutes reviewing and reading the material we could understand of the text had actually been hours. We were surprised when my mother came to the door of the room saying we needed to get ready for dinner. She had spoken to the Tripps, and David was free to come along if he wished—which of course he did. We were going to the Grill Room at the Hotel Taft. It was a place we frequently dinned over the weekend. A place where we could listen to Vincent Lopez and his Orchestra—a friend through Father's music publisher brother Barney.

We showed Mother the notebook and related our adventure. She expressed no major outward concern but said, "I see." Something about our story clearly was troubling.

She frowned and said, "I need to discuss your adventure with Father and won't be surprised if he has lots of questions for the three of you." Scanning the pages, she became excited. "What a remarkable discovery," she said. "This is something that would likely require a variety of minds to fully understand." Tempering her enthusiasm and regaining her composure, she said, "But for now we need to get ready for dinner."

CHAPTER 15

THE TAFT

THE TAFT was a fairly large hotel for its time stretching a block from 50th to 51st Street on Seventh Avenue. Architecturally, it appeared a mixture of Rococo, Italian Renaissance and Empire Period. It was also a mixed-function structure as the southeast corner of the building also served as the lobby for the Roxy Theatre.

Lopez was one of the Big Band greats. His fame had grown rapidly when his orchestra was an impromptu fill-in for an early radio broadcast. When asked to announce his own orchestra, as the announcer had not shown up on time, approaching the microphone he said disarmingly, "Hello everybody, Lopez speaking." That became his hallmark opening: "Lopez speaking"—frequently followed by his band playing "Nola," another one of his hallmarks. But Vincent wasn't just a bandleader and a remarkably accomplished pianist. He, like Houdini, was multifaceted and smart, with a myriad of interests. Interests and subjects that might have seemed far-fetched—like astrology and numerology. To our group, he fit right in. As I came to understand, he was "one of us."

Lopez's influence on music and musicians spanned many years. Names that began their star track under his wing included, among others, Glenn Miller, Betty and Marion Hutton, the Dorsey brothers, and Artie Shaw.

When we arrived at the Taft, we found Artie Shaw listening to the music and seated alone at a large table in a circular booth near the band. Barney, Father's brother, had published many of the numbers popularized by Shaw's band The Gramercy Five.

Recognizing my folks from previous introductions, Artie motioned for us to join him. He told us he was visiting the States, in from his new home in Spain. While on business in New York he had stopped by the Taft, as many often did, to hear Vincent's latest musicians.

Seeing us approaching Shaw's table, Vincent had his orchestra strike up "Mucho de Nada"—a Latin number once popularized by Shaw and published by Barney. As strains of the melody played, we sat down with Artie. Nearly simultaneously our first drinks arrived as the waiter was familiar with our crowd. My father had his typical Manhattan, I noted three instead of the usual two cherries he was given. One each, of course, for me and Cheryl but the waiter was clever enough to note the presence of David as well. My mother was given a Whiskey Sour—also with cherries. Of course, David, Cheryl, and I were given a standard grenadine mixture in ginger ale complete with a cherry skewered on the end of a plastic sword ... Cheryl's drink sported a small paper-and-wood umbrella on its side. The closest we were going to get to a Rob Roy was a Roy Rogers or the girl's version, a Shirley Temple. Better than alcohol to us, we'd be eating a lot of cherries, a child's aperitif to a meal.

Between ordering dinner and the arrival of our food, my parents had taken to the dance floor and Shaw, apparently unable to resist, had taken up a clarinet and had joined the band for a few numbers of this particular set.

Still seated at the table, but now without the adults, I noticed a change in the air, not quite a chill, more like a breeze and the music, now strains of Shaw's "Summit Ridge Drive," followed by the band playing "The Hornet," seemed to pulse louder. David and Cheryl must have had the same sensations for Cheryl abruptly said, "He's here. It reminds me of Halloween when he came to us. I can feel him."

We looked around and saw a figure uniquely familiar seated at the bar. Holding a tall drink in his left hand, a well-dressed gentleman with curly dark hair sat erect, regarding the bandleader. David pulled at my sleeve as he also said, "Cheryl, Cheryl," while motioning with his head towards the bar. The music continued even louder in our heads as all of us realized that it was Houdini sitting there, absorbing the music and the atmosphere and waiting for us to notice him. Then, sensing our stares, Houdini's deep brown eyes came to rest on us, his head nodding in acknowledgment of our mutual awareness of the others' presence.

He reached into his inner coat pocket for pen and paper and then appeared to be writing. Within a short time, he folded the paper and put it down. A moment later David, looking down on the table, grabbed a folded piece of paper that suddenly appeared in front of him. Opening it, there were two sentences scrawled across. It read: "VIII is complete. To see clearly is Divine."

"Argh," David said. "Another riddle. Houdini said there were rules he didn't fully understand. But what is he telling us now?"

Cheryl responded, "Right, I think we should go talk to him." But looking up and back to the bar, he had vanished. Had he walked out or just dematerialized? The music had also stopped and my parents, along with Artie and Vincent, were returning to the table.

This was the late 1950s and Artie had already published his autobiographical *The Trouble with Cinderella*. Music had already become more a part of his past life than present. His playing music for us today was an anachronistic treat. He had clandestinely been a part of The Inner Circle for many years. Brilliant but somewhat self-centered, married too many times to count, he had already left the band world many times.

His current intellectual pursuit was higher mathematics involving such obscure problems as the Reimann Hypothesis ... an unsolved problem with implied results about the distribution of a prime number. Well, at least we had already learned about prime numbers in school, but why would anyone so talented as a musician leave that to study math? That was exactly why Artie was "one of us." He had special talents far beyond those of playing the clarinet in a style that often left his sometime nemesis, Benny Goodman, to wonder.

All intellectual equals in their often esoteric manner, Artie belonged to the group.

The conversation with Artie somehow breezed over his numerous marriages to Hollywood starlets and sometimes vacuous beings to the more serious matters at hand.

Though the conversation often came back to him, he was still more than willing to be involved and offer up his math knowledge. He was made aware of the new material we had at hand and of the importance and necessity of its deciphering while preserving the information only for those within our inner circle. He didn't know how Houdini was in our midst but he was now aware that an awesome puzzle piece, potentially of immense power, was in our hands, Houdini's notebook.

Still in the city for the weekend and coming to join in for the evening, Walter and Litzka—China Boy in tow— came walking through the Taft's Grill Room door. Once at the table, it wasn't long before Litzka and Vincent were conversing about numerology and things were settling down as dinner was served to the table. Ending his break and having now had a quick bite to eat ,Vincent returned to the band only to be replaced at the table by another individual David, Cheryl, and I did not know.

There are good people and there are bad people. Then there are also just evil people.

From what we had gleaned so far, Houdini's notebook discussed the seven or eight categorical forms of magic or manipulation of matter that could be accomplished as a learned skill. There were other forces or powers too—all within the realms of natural science—that are genetically passed from one generation to the next or acquired in a new generation through genetic mutation. These were heightened intuitive skills, foreknowledge, and interpretive powers. This is what Litzka used and had spoken to David and me about in my father's library when examining our palms. Those with the right skills could read the outward signs of such ability. Litzka was able to read our genetic lines in our palms—the morphologic evidence that mentally we (including Litzka) had innate abilities to sense things. And so, when evil walked through the door of the Grill Room approaching our table many of us were sensing it and looking in its direction.

The Grill Room, geographically not too far from Grand Central Station, was often like Grand Central in that people crossed paths there to and from events, stopping in briefly or for hours for a beer, a snack, or a meal while simultaneously taking in the entertainment and the fun and the frenzy. Given our location it could have been happenstance alone that brought this individual into our midst at this time—or it could have been more than a coincidence that he should have arrived while we were there.

My mother greeted him as she would any friend or acquaintance, belaying little of the inner awareness she and we were feeling. An unexpected and likely unwanted guest, through social convention alone she motioned for him to take the seat that Vincent recently had filled.

Across from us now, there was someone who otherwise physically would have passed as a kindly, older gentleman. True he was thin with quite white, somewhat translucent appearing skin, mustached, and with very long pale hands. But he was nevertheless distinguished and finely dressed, not at all out of place for this part of town, wearing a jacket, waistcoat, and a loosely tied black bow tie. His left gloved hand rested on the head of a walking stick. As he began removing the glove, there was another sign of his character, however. On the fourth finger from his thumb, he wore an exceptional ring—two snakes intertwined, holding rubies in their mouths.

Cheryl whispered to us, "Is it my imagination or is he surrounded by a red cloud? Oh darn it, I guess it was just my imagination," she said, as the red cloud had vanished for her. "But take a look at his hands."

Normally David and I would not have paid much attention to the stranger who had joined our group but following Cheryl's comment, we looked across the table and saw the familiar snakes which now appeared to be, and likely in reality were, writhing around his finger. The ring bore an uncanny resemblance to the one worn by the stranger who had held us captive in our lobby vestibule earlier in the day. This piqued our interest enough that we were straining to hear over other conversations at the table as to exactly what he was talking about to our mother. Unfortunately, only David was able to hear a few words here and there as Cheryl and I also struggled to hear the conversation. But this is what was being said:

"You know Chesley, I've come across something you and Morris would be interested in."

"Oh, really Robert. And what might that be?"

Robert, clearly for effect, reacted by slowly reaching into his inside jacket pocket to bring out a gold, no doubt Dunhill, cigarette case. With one hand he opened the case while his other hand sought one of the filter-tipped cigarettes it held. Bringing the cigarette to his lips he closed the case, carefully placing it back into his pocket. Reaching for a lighter within his side pocket he brought it up and lit it with one click, simultaneously lighting the end of the cigarette. Inhaling deeply, he blew out a long plume of silver-gray smoke. He knew what my dad really wanted. Looking slyly first at my mom and then my father, his lips pursed with a wry smile before he spoke a little louder saying, "A Petrus von Rosenheim."

Petrus von Rosenheim was a thirteenth-century monk whose early writings on the science of memory would make a stellar addition to the memory collection my dad was now forming.

"Yes? Now how did you manage to find one of those? I must admit you definitely have my undivided attention," Father replied.

Robert pulled out the chair that had been Vincent's and sat down. Facing the mirrored backdrop of the circular banquette, his attention was briefly diverted to admire his own reflection. He noticed the ends of his mustache were awry. With both hands, he gave a slight twist trying to curve the ends upward in a Dali-like manner. He had a face you would never forget.

As he spoke, he continued to admire the image that only he could see of himself reflecting back in the mirror. The image was one of a rodent. He raised a paw-like hand and swept back the thinning hair across the top of his head.

"Well, Chesley, Morris, I'm not at liberty to share the provenance with you at this time but as you know they are very, very rare, and this one's a manuscript. Fourteen hundreds. Vellum. It could be a keystone for your new collecting interest in memory."

So he was a book dealer (along with being a part of the other group, something only hinted at by all of our mutual unease)—one of those often intellectual yet unusual individuals who acquaint themselves with subjects that are of esoteric interest. Generally knowledgeable in many areas themselves, a dealer would match interests between the personalities of buyers and sellers. A sale frequently revolved around a peculiar dance.

Price was not always the only thing on the table. Sellers might withhold an item for sale should the buyer appear unworthy or inappropriate. The 1950s were still a time when a buyer's provenance could be as important to a seller as an item's provenance could be to a buyer.

Robert's eyes rested now squarely on my father when he spoke, trying to pigeonhole him into a mark.

My father's ears perked up with the talk of manuscripts. After the magic collection moved to Washington, my parents' interests in the science of memory and mnemonics took over and the apartment was rapidly filling again with texts on these subjects. My father was an astute purchaser of manuscripts and early printings of subjects he collected.

Nothing Robert could say or do would sway him from playing the hand of a knowledgeable collector, no matter the offering. He was no one's "mark."

"Well, you will have to tell us more," Dad spoke as his attention, along with Walter's, turned towards the uninvited guest.

Litzka, on the other hand, moved from her position and came to join us at the inner side of the circular table.

"I know you all feel it too. He is not the nice man he appears to be, is he? But your parents have obviously had some dealings with him before." She paused for a loud refrain of music before continuing. "I think he has come here to see that you, and I mean all of you, are here. Clearly an effort is being made to keep up with the whereabouts of the notes you found."

How did Litzka know we had found the book? Did she know we had actually seen Houdini and that he had just been here? How did Father McKeen know? And how did the man in the lobby at home know what we had?

Even with Robert across the table, I had to ask her. The sound of the music, I hoped, would be enough to hinder comprehension of the conversation at our side of the circle from being overheard by Robert sitting directly opposite on the outer circle.

Listening to my flood of questions, Litzka asked for us to come with her. Litzka was not a small woman but neither was she very tall. Nevertheless, standing by the table with Robert seated, she appeared ever so much taller than Robert and made me realize that Robert was indeed a small man.

Bringing China Boy, she proceeded to take us out of the Grill Room and into the main lobby of the Taft. At this hour the lobby was more subdued and hushed with its honeycombed ceiling, Persian carpets, leather seats, and potted palms. Typical of this period hotel, there was a balconied mezzanine where she could talk to us in relative privacy and quiet. It was to there we followed her.

"I was wondering when you would start asking questions. So much has happened so quickly, and Walter and I have had so few trips to the city recently to visit you, your parents, and our other friends."

China Boy, who had become a little restless, received some attention from Litzka's left hand while she continued. "First off, Father Bruce has spoken to me to let me know he has been in contact with you"—and with a wry smile she said—not everything is by magic, you know." And then turning to China Boy she interjected, "That's a good boy," while stroking his feathered back. "I know about Houdini's notes you found because of him. He knew because Houdini told him. Not in person though. There was a paper he found on his desk that Houdini had left, informing him he had succeeded in returning. But there were conditions Houdini only partially understood—something to do with conservation of energy—and that you children were chosen as his contacts because of your abilities and connections—that these things allowed maximum conservation of energy. Apparently, this return will only last until a set amount of energy has been transformed, and that's it, he will be gone again. So, all of you are key to helping him do whatever he needs to do, and he must accomplish it with minimal expenditure of energy."

David interrupted here and said, "That's it, that is why he is speaking in riddles at times. They are condensed directions. If we can understand and solve them, we have saved him expenditure of energy."

"Of course," Cheryl said, realizing David was right. "I think you've hit on it."

To my other questions, those dealing with the man in our home lobby and how he knew we had the book she had one simple answer, *spies*. China Boy, always the show bird, cockled, emphasizing her one-word response.

Litzka then sought to explain a portion of the history of The Inner Circle and The Outer Circle, the universal struggle between forces of good and evil, and how "destiny," if you will call it such, was locked into this ongoing battle. A battle as old as time itself where The Inner Circle continued to guard the centuries of advanced knowledge for applications regarding the general good of mankind while The Outer Circle sought to increase their possession of such knowledge and skills for their own aggrandizement and power.

She explained that McKeen had left the book in our hands not only to hone our skills but also because we were part of what was necessary to unravel its secrets.

Litzka, with her own set of genetically imbued skills, understood that in timelines, some things are immutable and must or will occur, and other things are "waiting to happen" by the course of events. Many events can occur that will change an individual's course in life but will not change the course of the universe. Some have theorized, though, that if enough good or bad occurs then a true universe change can occur. But that is only a theory she emphasized. Nevertheless, that was why it was so important the group of the Inner Circle continued to protect the knowledge of the centuries as it related to controlling matter and the forces of nature.

As evidence of the potential possibility for a universal change for evil, Robert sat nearby in the Grill Room conversing, waiting, and watching.

"It's complicated," is a refrain often heard about life. And, well, this was complicated. There were the various players interwoven in our lives, the good and the bad. And how many synonyms are there for the word *good* versus the word *bad*. With bad we can substitute evil, vile, repugnant, atrocious, abominable. There just are not enough words to substitute for truly bad. But then there are perhaps equally too few but more words to substitute for the word "good" ...

wonderful, ace, stupendous, admirable, splendid, superlative, or hyphenations like tip-top or super-excellent.

And that is why we are frequently left with the phrase "good versus evil." It comes down to that, with too few words to describe anything other.

CHAPTER 16

AND WHILE WE WERE AT THE TAFT ...

NIGEL, EARTHA Kitt's pet boa constrictor, made ready to leave the penthouse where he resided when he was not out perusing his surroundings. He understood that Eartha's kitties were off-limits. She had trained him well in that respect and was most generous about providing fresh rodents from a pet supply store for his diet. However, he still preferred both kitties and pigeons.

There really was quite an abundance of both of his favorites if one were vigilant and knew the right hunting grounds. Pigeons loved the rooftop garden that Eartha tended to. And there were also residents foolish enough to actually put food out on their courtyard windowsills to attract pigeons as well. Extra snacks were only a question of being in the right place at the right time. It certainly helped that his mistress, being in the performance world, was frequently out. But even when she was at home, Nigel rarely received the adoring attention, probably because he wasn't what one might normally choose as a free-roaming house pet. You see, honestly, Eartha seemed to prefer the company of her cats when she was at home. Nigel just seemed appropriate to her as an accouterment, just not so much a pet to lavish attention on. So, there he was, often neglected. Nigel led a very solitary life with little amusement aside from his hunting.

To date, there had only been one close call for him. His pigeon game had almost been discovered when the residents of the building had started to find feathers in their drinking water. Unfortunately, there had been that one crazy bird. Thinking to escape Nigel, the bird had flown into an inadvertently left-open portion of the lid of the building's water tank. The tank's rooftop position provided the proper water pressure for the apartments below. Louis, the building superintendent, had made quite a fuss spending several days inspecting the rooftop area until he found the remains of the bird which had become trapped within ... the yucky source of the feathers that intermittently had begun to flow along with water coming out of apartment taps. Nigel's rodent consumption went up during that time but Eartha failed to make a connection.

The penthouse, having been an afterthought and not part of the original design of Glen Cairn, had not been terribly solidly constructed. There were numerous openings and Nigel was able to access them to gain his freedom. He must've thought *thank goodness*, as this and Eartha's nonchalance regarding her habitat had given him free rein of the house and much of the rest of Glen Cairn.

Over the course of time, Nigel became quite adept at using the window ledges along the courtyard walls as a base to launch himself from. The eighth floor was one of his favorite hunting places.

A certain Mrs. Donovan lived alone there in her eight-room apartment. Alone, that is, except for an unknown number of cats. She herself had stopped keeping count. The place reeked of cat and there were open food tins and water dishes all over the place.

Not that Nigel had been inside to visit, but he could see in through the windows as he waited hopefully to launch himself from one ledge to the next should a kitten venture out. And they did venture out. Mrs. Donovan left the windows ajar year-round (perhaps to air out the pungent smell). A small feline taking a nap on an outside window-sill ledge became something yummy for Nigel to fill his belly with. So much better than letting a poor feline soul accidentally tumble down eight floors to a wasted demise *n'est-ce pas*?

Between the Donovan cats and the pigeon population, it truly was a wonder that his mistress Eartha had not noticed the reduction in the expense account for rodents from what it had been during the first few months after she had taken him in.

Eartha's boa Nigel had been approached by another serpent, Milo, who appeared as if by magic while Eartha was out. Milo introduced himself and enlisted his help in a very sensitive reptilian brotherhood matter. Apparently, there was an item The Outer Circle required and it was located in the Youngs' apartment on the eighth floor. Since they knew that Nigel was a pro at recognizance at Glen Cairn, they were enlisting him. His compensation for the completion of his mission would be three kitties and four pigeons. How could he resist?

The auspicious handcuffs, Houdini's link to another world, a fourth dimension as it were, still sat open and silent on their library shelf within the apartment. They were sequestered behind a pair of sliding glass doors of shelves meant for display. The feature added protection from dust while at the same time emphasizing an item's importance.

For years quantum physicists postulated the existence of other dimensions of time and space as the only way to fully explain the peculiarities of particle physics. This of course, another dimension, was the explanation as to where Houdini had been after his apparent death. Somehow those handcuffs were a link to that other world.

The benefits of being able to freely move between dimensions was not only enticing but also potentially useful in so many ways. The possibility of disappearing for years and then returning nearly unchanged? If time were involved, then to return younger, or older, at whim? And what other miraculous diabolical contrivances existed in that other world? Might they be useful here too?

As it were, The Outer Circle's discussion about the cuffs led to this current plan where Milo was sent to see about retrieving the cuffs for their benefit. Milo in turn enlisted Nigel.

In this particular scheme concocted by Milo and Nigel, Nigel gradually made his way down from the penthouse via the window ledges in his normal manner and reached the Youngs' residence, adjacent to Mrs. Donovan's. With hopeful expectation, he glanced longingly at Mrs. D's window ledge. Unfortunately, there were no snacks waiting. In a way that was all for the best since he had a mission to accomplish.

Thank goodness the window was ajar in the room he had been directed to. The room was also fortunately empty of human inhabitants. Nigel slithered in and made his way to the Handcuffs visible on a shelf, just as Milo had described. What Milo was not aware of though was the presence of the glass doors. Nigel was able to launch himself towards the cuffs from the table top nearby but after several head butts he failed at opening the glass and the cuffs remained stubbornly within. There was no way to reach the targeted handcuffs as they were soundly being kept out of his reach by the sturdy glass-enclosed case.

Nigel recognized defeat and that the mission would have to be aborted. The plan had been for him to slither into the cuffs and then exit through the window. There was no way he could transport the cuffs along with their housing.

He knew Milo would be most disappointed, but then Milo had neglected to mention the heavy glass doors protecting the cuffs. There would be no tasty kittens and pigeons for him today unless he was able to catch something himself.

Reluctantly, he took one last glance at the well-protected cuffs so well displayed. So close, yet so unattainable. Turning back, he slithered through the window glancing as he went at Mrs. D's ledge just in case he might be in luck, but no luck there either. He started his descent to the lobby of the courtyard, where he would soon rendezvous with his fellow reptilian brother and relay the news of his failed mission.

CHAPTER 17

THE CODE ROOM

WHEN I awoke Sunday morning the sky was once again a dazzling clear blue. The day's eastern sun's rays brightly bathed the park along with the Jersey Shore across the Hudson. I had only a moment glancing out the living room windows before I realized, rubbing sleep from my eyes, that many people were scattered about the room.

After we returned home last night and had gone to sleep, my mother must have discussed the notebook find with my father. They apparently had gotten right to work assembling a troop of locals from The Inner Circle as decoders and decipherers as there were people scattered about various rooms of our apartment studying the separated leaves of Houdini's work. These were some of the people who made the world turn 'round.

Most were rarely the focus of a front-page story but some were. As I was coming to learn, many were also responsible for the great happenings of humans. Affairs of state, nations being born, wars being won, advances occurring in science, some of those individuals responsible were now in this room. The source of much of the good in the world originated through the machinations of members of The Inner Circle.

Sometimes it is difficult to see history being made but it was clear that it was, and it was happening here at Glen Cairn. There was the hushed buzzing sound of discussions taking place. The tension was as palpable as the sound of bees within a hive surrounded me as I walked among them. They were working to elucidate what had been written within the binding containing Houdini's writings.

Knowing that there was only a limited time that Houdini might be present to help decipher his writings, albeit not necessarily in person, a decision was made by my parents and the Gibsons to bring together 'at hand' members of he Inner Circle to assist with the process. The atmosphere was one brimming with expectant and electric but not unpleasant energy. Already awake, David and Cheryl were part of the gathering that had continued through the night and into this next day.

I recognized Mrs. Roosevelt sitting in the large yellow wing-backed chair by the living room window. As it could easily accommodate the two of us, David and I frequently chose to share the seat when we scanned the skies searching for extraterrestrial aircraft. I had only met her once, and briefly at that, when she had visited our class one day at the United Nations International School. She had stopped to speak with me and then a few others as she went around greeting the children. When I came home and told my mother who had visited that day, she had said, "oh, I'm so glad you had a chance to meet Eleanor. I remember the first time I met her." Then, she continued telling the story of how she came to meet her during World War II while she was at Fort Oglethorpe.

At that time my mother had finished her basic training and training as a cryptographer and was now a captain with the signal corps in the WAAC. Through some bureaucratic snafu she had been assigned to the post as a photographer ("Sounded like cryptographer," she said, "a typical Army snafu"). When she arrived, although she insisted she was a cryptographer, Oglethorpe didn't have a use for a cryptographer so she was temporarily forced to take on a position she did not want: the job of the camp photographer. With that mandate, she rapidly mastered the necessary skills. Cryptography was her interest—and the area where she knew she could be most useful to the Allied effort. Nevertheless, she continued to have difficulty getting her commanding officer to rectify the snafu and move her on to where she could apply her cryptographic skills.

President Roosevelt and the WAAC commander at Fort Oglethorpe

As she told the story, early one morning on her way to breakfast she noticed a lady standing, suitcase in hand, looking this way and that, apparently unfamiliar with the campgrounds. Approaching to help, she recognized the lady as Mrs. Roosevelt. The First Lady had arrived to rendezvous with Franklin, who was scheduled to review the WAAC training at Oglethorpe.

Asking if she could give directions, Mrs. Roosevelt wanted to know if she could point her to the infirmary. My mother answered that the infirmary was not open so early in the morning. Then she asked Mrs. Roosevelt if she'd had breakfast. Not having eaten yet, Mrs. Roosevelt was more than happy to accompany my mother to the officer's mess hall instead. There they sat, like old buddies, talking and having a good time. Both of them were good at that, talking in an easy-going manner and making friends fast. Well, when my mother's commanding officer came in, my mother stood up and said, "Good morning, sir, I'd like to introduce you to my friend Mrs. Roosevelt." Of course, her commanding officer leaped to the conclusion that she and Mrs. Roosevelt had been friends for some time, as their intimate banter and the fact that they were having break-fast together gave that impression.

Soon after, when my mother wanted a transfer to make use of her cryptographer skills, her commanding officer, still believing my mother was good friends with Mrs. Roosevelt, quickly obliged. Thus began her assignment as a cryptographer to the British overseas, one that she alluded had links to compatriots working at Bletchley Park, the at the time top-secret home to British codebreakers. She remained a distant but intermittent friend of the First

Lady. With the recent memory of meeting her at school crossing my mind, the First Lady looked up briefly and smiled as if acknowledging not only my presence but also her fondness for my mother and their shared past. It did not cross my mind until a decade or so later but I eventually wondered how much the government knew of the two circles and who within the government, present and past, was aware of the existence of such groups and their relative influences on events nationally and internationally.

There was always the future to think about and, with the nascent awareness of our true natures for Cheryl, David, and me, this was all just beginning.

Continuing to scan the room I saw other familiar faces. Present, and apparently called into action were: Harry Blackstone, Eli Wallach, Phil Davis (an applied mathematician and cousin of my father from New England who would ultimately be awarded the Chauvenet Prize), Umberto Eco, and Artie Shaw. Artie and Phil were clearly deeply involved, discussing the mathematical significance of some of the formulas in Houdini's notebook. Others in the group, led by Eco, appeared to be working on problems posed by the symbolic logic that made appearances here and there within the text. Symbols staring up from pieces of paper. Everywhere people were busy working with speed and purpose mixed with intermittent sounds of pencil points snapping, occasionally becoming broken as they scratched and erased across sheets of paper.

Ultimately there was the shuffling of many pages, gradually assimilating, becoming collated into a work comprehensible to all.

My mother, acting as chief cryptographer, had organized the group by their particular skills; some particularly unique, all to help unravel whatever information they could from Houdini's writings. These first studies of his notes would be cataloged to form the beginnings of a series of writings and "translations," if you will, of particular parts of the text. Any areas that were unclear or remained stalwart against our combined skills would be duly recorded separately in the hopes that Houdini himself would at some point be able to enlighten us as to his discoveries and methods.

Watching her now, she was in charge. I felt a child's pride seeing their mother in this role as code master. An attractive woman, her brown hair was perfectly styled and accentuated what I thought were her best facial features—high cheekbones and a fine, thin nose. She made quite a figure moving with grace and purpose from one decipherer to the next. At times, seeing a potential solution, she even offered reference books from the resources of our home cryptographical library. For a moment, in my mind, she appeared in uniform, much like photos she had shown me from her scrapbook from World War II.

Chesley Virginia Barnes-Young, in uniform, at her desk when a cryptologist with the WACs.

Some of those photos were remarkable as she had been one of the few American women the master Italian pioneer of fashion photography, Arturo Ghergo, had asked to pose for his iconic photographic records of wartime American female participants.

Both sporting steel-rimmed glasses, I watched my father and Walter in Dad's study as they assiduously worked as a team as they would on many of their co-authored books to come. The study was dark with only a single standing lamp and a desk lamp illuminating materials. They sat at Dad's desk with books scattered about and some of the drawers indiscriminately ajar. Listening briefly to the discussion, their minds simultaneously seemed to light up with eureka moments after having gone over what appeared to be a difficult passage. Then, in conversation, they would quickly hit ideas back and forth like a ball in a game of ping pong until one or the other came to an eureka conclusion on their own.

In the hexagon rooms of Borges's "Library of Babel," there was to be a "crimson hexagon," a space holding in literary form books that were "all-powerful"—perhaps the keys of understanding of all knowledge. To some extent, now, I believe we were all hoping that in these writings of Houdini we might have in a single text a "crimson hexagon" to add to all the other writings protected by The Inner Circle.

There were some stumbling blocks both in the deciphering and in the interpretations. Eli and Phil were able to appropriately work through the Cyrillic and other somewhat obscure writings in Eastern European languages as well as the symbolic logic. Others present were able to decipher the pictographs. Nonetheless, throughout the text there were portions that did not appear to make sense. In a yet-to-be-identified code, a letter or number would appear as a series of colored dots, as if a peculiar form of rubric making. The visible letter or number on its own when plugged into a particular formula ultimately did not work.

Eli, moving again to work with Harry Blackstone continued to work on this. They appeared stumped until David joined them and helped. While they were discussing one of the letters as a possible "F" David interrupted and said, "I don't see an 'F,' I see an 'R.'"

They both said "Where?" And David showed them, but they still saw only an "F." Showing David the rest of the "rubrics" he continued to identify letters or numbers as different than what the others could see.

In David's case, "solving" the code required an inborn special trait he was exhibiting. For this case it was an ability; it was his genetics and a red-green color deficiency in his vision! Something many blithely call one of the forms of color blindness. Either Houdini had this particular form of vision and color deficiency and knowingly had used it to his advantage to further obfuscate his multilayers of coded text, or had figured a way to replicate and exploit such anomalies of nature. Eli, calling to the other room for my dad to come over, hoped Dad might explain the visual disparities. My dad as an ophthalmologist rapidly recognized why David was seeing what he was and said, "David is right. David clearly has a form of color deficiency." Houdini's use of this perception difference gave him yet another clever way to mask a code within a code.

It took my father as an ophthalmologist to realize that Houdini had protected some of the key numbers and letters in his formulas by obscuring them from those with *normal* color vision, making them visible only to those with red-green color deficiencies.

Houdini had turned that deficiency into an asset.

Cheryl, observing David's color interpretations, realized for the first time that she was apparently what my father described as a synesthestic grapheme—a genetic trait more common in women and far less prevalent than those with color deficiencies. Looking at the passages of Houdini's work that had seemed like meaningless compilations of words were actually strings of short instructions to her, synesthetically encoded in the sentence. As father related, synesthesia manifests itself in individuals in a variety of forms. For Cheryl, certain letters were visualized in her brain as if they were printed in a particular color. Predominantly green words within a sentence when picked out and placed sequentially became the final instruction to complete a particular equation or method.

And then there were a series of pages Eleanor determined to be a palimpsest wherein material within the original writing, elucidated through the impressions on the paper, were required to fully unravel the meanings of material written on top of it.

Still there remained one totally enigmatic area of the text: VIII.

Houdini had said in his message delivered to David at the Grill Room in the Hotel Taft: "VIII is complete. To see clearly is Divine." But no matter the method tried to view the invisible, the blank pages remained just that—blank.

Though the group was making progress, the day had worn on. David and I could barely keep our eyes open and Cheryl had faded hours before. As the search through the references of my mother's library and her personal skill finally became exhausted the sun was setting on the Jersey side across the river and it was time for all to get some rest.

Walter said, "I think it's time to call it a day. It might be inspirational if a small group of us continued working on this at my home in Maine next weekend. I have several books Houdini gave me that may help us with this. Why don't some of my séance cohorts come up Friday night?"

"I don't know, Walter," Artie said. "Up in Maine, you may find what we're looking for to figure this all out. But I have a feeling we may need to do some work using the library under the cathedral." And Mrs. Roosevelt agreed. So, Eleanor and Artie suggested that should the visit to Walter's leave us without a solution on how to visualize what must be on the seemingly blank pages in VIII, then enlisting the aid of Father McKeen and accessing the resources housed so far beneath the ground was the place to go. Perhaps those texts held the answer. Perhaps Houdini was directing us there, to the subterranean archive of the Cathedral of St. John the Divine when he wrote: "To see clearly is Divine." And it would be there the eighth form would become complete.

CHAPTER 18

UNIS

THE WEEK went by slowly. The week went by fast.

Yes, it can do both.

A nearly full daytime moon hung in the Monday morning sky, adding to the bluish light that engulfed us as Cheryl, David, and I waited for the school bus that would take us across town to the United Nations International School (UNIS). As we waited, I think all three of us were still groggy and in the process of waking up, individually thinking over the activities of the past weekend.

I had never really thought too much about why or just how a handful of kids from the States were students at such a school. Now, it did seem to make a bit more sense. Being part of a group of internationals, many of whom were there because of their parents having functions at the United Nations, had seemed peculiar. Thinking about the events of that weekend, about what Litzka had revealed, and about Mrs. Roosevelt so recently visiting my class and spending time talking with me and other children, I started to suspect that quite a few classmates and other students might also be offspring of parents associated with the Inner Circle in countries around the globe. What special powers we and all of them might possess was a thought beginning to run through my mind. The occurrences of the past few days had been so full there had been little time for me to consider all the happenings let alone their implications. The same was apparently true for both Cheryl and David. As my wakefulness returned, I wanted to discuss this with them but the school bus was hardly the place to have a guarded conversation. That would have to wait until lunchtime recess.

Classes at UNIS during that period were held in a turn-of-the-century three-story red brick and sandstone building that used to be run as a public school by the City of New York. It had been closed by the city for many years. The administrators of UNIS had arranged to rent the structure from the city until they could complete a new building at the edge of Manhattan on the East River. On the current building's outside walls there were still stone engraved signs indicating separate entrances for "Boys" and "Girls." Those entrances were no longer used and, instead, all entered through the main entrance, which included a central grand stairway of stone stairs and risers with ornate newel posts, wooden banisters, and cast-iron supports.

The first landing was flanked by stairs on each side leading to the next level. At the center of the landing, there were double doors leading to administrative offices and classrooms. The ground floor area consisted of the lunchroom, indoor gym, locker rooms, bathrooms, and additional classrooms toward an annex at the rear of the building. The center of the building enclosed an outdoor courtyard used for recess activities.

Classroom desks were individual wood and iron pieces bolted to the wooden floors where the seat could fold up and the desktop could be raised so one might store their books within. Each desk had a now-unused area for the student to place a bottle of ink for use with the ink pens our earlier counterparts employed.

I don't recall too much about many of our classmates but none were ever cruel or bullying in any way that children can be. Those in the older classes had always seemed more than willing to offer guidance, encouragement, and a comradery-like presence to younger schoolmates. Those mannerisms in and of themselves suggested to me that all or most of us were from similar backgrounds, though we were certainly separated by our different cultures and countries of origin. But then, there was an incident occurring on that particular day that made me think that perhaps the school also taught some or many children from families belonging to the Outer Circle.

Here is what happened. Each classroom also had a cloakroom, a place to store our winter coats with hooks on the walls, spaces below for our boots, and another for our lunch bag or box. At morning recess, as the class was led out to the yard by our teacher, Miss Swensen, I remembered I left a snack I had brought that I'd planned on sharing with David once we were outdoors. I decided to hang back to the end of the line as our class filed out through the classroom door. Quickly, I went to the cloakroom to retrieve the snack. While I was squatting down, rifling through my lunch bag, the door to the cloakroom suddenly closed.

Next, I heard the click of the lock latch. That was followed by the ceiling light going off. I don't know why but I stifled my desire to cry out, "Hey, someone's in here. Open the door." I suppose I feared it was no accident but someone on the other side who had shut the door, locked me in, and turned out the light. They wanted me locked in and disoriented. The door had two opaque glass panes on its upper half, allowing light to filter through. Though frightened, I crept towards the door as silently as I could. On the other side, the motionless dim outline of a person was visible to me. My heart was now pounding as I stood breathless inside, wondering whether to scream, "Let me out," or for some reason to remain silent and act like perhaps I wasn't in there at all. Then I heard footsteps approaching and two people began talking. I couldn't make out everything they said though the few words I could hear increased my fear. "They're bringing the van around ... Have you something to keep him quiet?

"No," they answered, "let me go get something." Then, there was quiet again with just that ghostly shadow against the window panes of the door. My panic rose. I was about to be kidnapped or worse. What else could those words mean? Shortly there were more sets of footsteps and louder voices. Relief came as first I heard Cheryl and then David talking and asking, "What are you doing here? You are not supposed to be here. You had better leave." There was a grunt. The shadow vanished and then the cloakroom door opened with both Cheryl and David standing there.

Cheryl said, "We wondered what was keeping you, and didn't want you to gobble up all of the snacks Mother had packed and figured you were up here doing just that. But also, David incidentally felt for his amulet and found it to be warm. He came to me and asked for me to check mine. It was warm too. That was all it took for us to know we had to come looking for you."

David followed with, "But golly, what a good thing. We sure didn't expect to find an upperclassman here keeping you locked in."

Cheryl asked, "What was this all about. Did he shove you in there? What happened? Do you know that boy?"

"I really think he and someone else were about to kidnap me," I exclaimed and then told them what I had heard. By then though, recess being brief, the class was returning and we had no more time to talk so Cheryl left to return to her class while David and I went to our desks.

At lunchtime recess, I was able to speak briefly with David and Cheryl regarding my thoughts that had been dawning on me as to the special nature of the school we attended. As it turned out, they too were harboring similar thoughts. With what had just occurred though, we each agreed to watch out for one another more than ever and to watch carefully during the week for any evidence that our schoolmates or teachers might be part of something bigger, something having nothing at all to do with school. It seemed clear to us that our find and possession of Houdini's notebook now also brought risk.

That afternoon rather than returning straight home from school David, Cheryl, and I decided to make a second visit to Father McKeen. After all, he had said he was there to help us learn about our powers. We still had to figure out what those powers might be. This time, Father McKeen was waiting for us on the church steps.

"How did you know we were coming?" I exclaimed. "Has Houdini been back in touch with you?"

"No, he has not. I know that you have come to talk with me about your special abilities and powers."

"How do you know that?" Cheryl asked.

"Well, I too have a special ability and that mine—" Father McKeen didn't finish the sentence out loud, rather we each heard him speaking within our own heads. He was telepathic and with his demonstration, we learned that so were we.

Following him inside and heading toward his office, we passed just a few parishioners seated in the pews. At this time of day, the church was mainly empty and the quiet within was broken only by the sound of our footsteps.

Once we were seated Father McKeen said, "Let me start with Cheryl's power first. Think back to when you were younger. I'll bet your mom has saved some of the drawings you made of your family from that time. I'm pretty sure you used a different color for your mom and your dad, yourself and brother. You weren't aware of it at the time but you did so as you were seeing their auras. Your teacher may not have understood the reason you chose those colors. Your parents may well have understood but if they never discussed it with you they probably weren't aware of it either. Seeing an aura is not a genetic trait but in some, it accompanies their synesthetic ability. With no formal training as you grew up, logic can get in its way causing the ability to fade."

"Oh my goodness," Cheryl said. "I totally understand what you're talking about. It was so strange when we were at the Taft with our family last night. A man who knew our parents joined us and I could have sworn he had a red cloud about him but when I asked David and Charlie if they saw it too, it no longer was there."

"Yes Cheryl, you really did see it and people often have a red aura when angry, and so I imagine that your parent's friend was displeased about something."

"You know," said David, "he was also wearing a ring we saw on another man who had been waiting for us in our lobby at home when returning from meeting you. The ring looked like two snake heads together with ruby-red eyes. He knew we had Houdini's notebook and he tried to have us turn it over to him."

"Ah," Father McKeen said, "the ring you saw is a symbol many wear who are part of the Outer Circle. But this is enough for today. You have homework and you should be on your way now."

Once home, I looked out from the living room windows overlooking the park and the river. Only two days had passed since the leaves were so full and bright on the trees and already the limbs of the trees stood nearly naked against the sky.

Everything that can be good can also be evil, that was something we were all about to learn if we did not know it already. The abruptness of this seasonal change brought this to mind.

Fall was clearly ending for me, for us, for Cheryl and David. The fall before the spring. The sharper winds of fall had prematurely begun to bring winter, stripping the leaves from trees. Hopefully they would give rise to an early spring as they gave rise to an early winter. All too soon the snow would be piling up against the entryways of the apartment buildings along the drive, snow driven by the winter winds coming off the Hudson.

That evening after finishing my homework I went to my father's study. Like all the other adults in our close-knit circle were doing this week, he was still working on the ciphers of Houdini's notebook. He sat with his head inclined toward the several books open before him and pages spread out over his desk. Were Houdini's writings just a grimoire of Sitra Achra, the writings of an anti-spiritualist and son of a rabbi, or was it something more?

At first Father did not notice me standing in the doorway waiting to be observed and given permission to enter. This was a time when he still smoked, usually a cigarette with which he could perform sleight of hand tricks, but he enjoyed a pipe as well. Now, a cigarette sat lit in an ashtray on his desk. I watched its smoke rising in ghost-like fashion through the air. Becoming aware of my presence, he looked up from his work and turned towards me as he reached for it, took a slow drag, then gave a Cheshire grin and caused the cigarette to vanish from his hand into thin air while blowing a smoke ring. I loved it when he would perform for me.

I was eager to better understand what Litzka had revealed to us.

Considering my father wise and wanting to be like him, I recall there were two times I asked him, "Did you ever feel you were as wise as your father?" Perhaps this was the first time. Maybe it was the second. At one time he had answered he had never felt as wise as his father, then at another time, he answered yes. What had happened in between? I should have asked him that too.

It would still be years before I read the works of Tillich, Homer, Sophocles, or Maimonides ... and realize that they too had been part of this, part of the Inner Circle. For now, I required only what a father could tell his son.

We talked and he tried to elucidate, to shed light on all that was transpiring. He made it easier for me to grasp what Cheryl, David, and I had recently learned about ourselves and the experiences that were unfolding before us. He said, "You are obviously laying the groundwork for a basic skill, but no one can tell which facet will ultimately be your favorite or which you will fully develop. You think I see things clearly ... but remember the fog never fully lifts, just that we, as adults, have had more bumps on the way and know how to tolerate them a little better and understand who we are, who we have become."

Good advice for most things in life, not just apropos to the experiences we were having now.

He added, "The way is never too easy ... and we must learn to ferret out the good that exists in any of us, thereby sustaining our own faith and egos. So, we work blindly for a while through sheer momentum, knowing that there must be more sunbeams ahead."

"And if we fail?" I asked.

"As for what's ahead, that's plenty. We don't expect anything startling or fantastic on your part; better, we'd like to see you derive personal satisfaction and pleasure from what you may be about. Mom and I are here as support and for many years will continue to assume most of the burden you may now feel; the responsibility which goes along with your abilities will grow with time. For now, for you, your sister, and David, it should just be a gradual and natural progression as you work together with us.

"Demands will grow with time but you will be prepared for them, of that I can assure you. You may find that no sooner than you wiggle out of one corner, another demand arises elsewhere. Don't discourage easily though. In fact, try to keep that word out of your vocabulary. Sooner then, all things will appear feasible!"

I was learning that our lives are shaped, encouraged, and motivated by our elders and past ancestors. Each of us plays a role in what becomes a familial generational epic tale.

CHAPTER 19

INTERLUDE

ON TUESDAY and for close to the rest of the week the moon
appeared full, and then nearly full as it sat visible in
the morning sky. The smell of freshly perked coffee and
toasted muffins hung in the air along with it, and with
a hint of bacon too as Mary had eggs, English muffins,
and crispy bacon ready for me, and coffee already made
for our parents. Cheryl, hating eggs, ate just a toasted
muffin with jam. We washed it all down with orange juice
prior to boarding the van that drove us, David, and other
West Side children cross-town to school. Our parents
left for work an hour earlier, Father for hospital rounds
and Mother for her teaching first graders at P.S. 125 in
Harlem. David's parents had been up and off at five to
be at the CBS Studios for the broadcasting of Paul's children's show *On the Carousel*.

At school, our teacher Miss Swenson discussed our
usual lessons but she also led the class in discussions
about current events ... Sputnik 1 and Sputnik 2 had
been launched. Space, science, and the possibility of the

unknown and other worlds were now realities. She was laying the groundwork for the impossible being possible. It was like we were observing the rituals of learning while no longer believing in all that we were taught.

CHAPTER 20

IS THERE A PHILOSOPHER IN THE HOUSE?

WHEN HOME again on Wednesday afternoon, I looked across the park from eight floors up and imagined the sycamores, Japanese cherry trees, and ginkgoes as they had been just a week before with golden leaves. Those leaves now lay about the streets or throughout the park in clumps or scattered here and there. They gave off their own peculiar smell of decay that somehow was also pleasant as the process led to a rebirth with new leaves after the winter months to come.

How was it that in life things could change so fast? And now I questioned everything taught in school and everyone in school ... the teachers, the students, relationships, who I was, my family and friend David. What powers would I find I had? How would those be used? What was I to do? It was scary, a bit unsettling. How could I be sure it was all a good thing and not a *bête noire*?

That evening I was awakened by Houdini's presence. It was thrilling to see him again.

I asked what he had been doing. He answered he had been spending much of his time deep within the Cathedral's hidden library, essentially searching for the Crimson Hexagon of Jorges Luis Borges ... the answer to every question, the making of order from disorder. He could then apply the knowledge to his own situation, his return to our time. But there was another problem he hinted about and one which seemed to make him nervous and almost a little fearful. It involved some physical difficulty, something that was occurring with greater frequency since his return. He did not explain exactly what that entailed, but the meaning of his comment would soon be revealed. As well, he expressed concern as to the directions and power the Outer Circle had come to develop of late, things of which I knew little about.

There was so much now I knew so little about.

At some time after midnight, having fallen asleep, I once again awoke. The house was quiet with everyone else asleep. I got up from bed and went from one room to the next walking through the hallways past the cabinets with curiosities and books and then found myself in my father's study. Houdini was sitting at my father's desk appearing as one might with a relaxed urbane comportment. He looked up with a wry expression on his face like someone paused in mid-thought, as if he himself was again questioning his presence within this time and space. This was indeed, in part, exactly what he had been doing.

"Why aren't you in bed?" he said.

"And why are you here?" I replied.

He cocked an eyebrow skyward, something within him acknowledging my own cockiness, such cockiness a trait

I was probably developing due to the unusual happenings of late.

After eyeing me for a few moments while I stood there expectantly, he said, "I'm still looking for some of the answers as to why I have returned here and now."

The recent events had had their impact on me and I was processing information at an alarming rate for my age so I answered, "You know my family and their friends, from what I understand, are part of The Inner Circle, and are working on making sense of your notebook, the writings you had us find."

"Yes, I'm aware of that. I believe it is critical they continue in their efforts. But I must continue to help them and they me. I had not realized the difficulties or importance of this battle between the factions ... between the two Circles. I am also afraid that my return will intensify the struggle. The formula I found ... I am afraid, it's about to create a major rift in the balance of powers. I came here this evening hoping something within your father's texts would show me how to correct the balance of powers my return has disrupted. Unfortunately, there is nothing here to help. It is more important now than ever that the group meet with me at the cathedral. You must make sure they are all there soon. But there are also other things to talk about."

"Like what?" I asked.

Houdini stood up from my father's desk chair and gazed about the room. The posters of past great stage magicians appeared as a backdrop to him as he spoke, a perfect Greek chorus lending visual support rather than words as emphasis to his words.

"Well, I know I have recognized that you, your friend David, and your sister are perplexed by the sudden revelations about your lives."

"Yes, that is true," I answered. "I know the three of us are bothered by everything we are learning."

"And you know ..." he continued, "I spent many years pushing myself to be disciplined through physical effort and mental effort. This I did by reading everything I could and at the same time pushing the limits of my physical strength. Becoming who I am was not inborn as it is for the three of you. More often one is a reflection of a part of where they are from rather than making of themselves that which they wish or were born to be."

Then he quoted T.S. Lawrence in saying: "All men dream Charlie, but not equally. Yes, it is not solely genetics wherein we can be a part of this eloquent group of the Inner Circle. Hard physical work and mastery over my body along with studies of texts on chemistry, physics, mathematics, philosophy ... reading, reading, reading led me to be able to ascertain some of our natures of existence. You cannot neglect your studies and become great or experience greatness. It requires more. Make no mistake about that! It is not enough to just dream about these things."

Then he quoted the rest of Lawrence's words: "'Those who dream by night in the dusty recesses of their minds wake up in the day to find it was vanity, but the dreamers of the day are dangerous men, for they may act their dreams with open eyes, to make it possible.'"

Finishing the quote, he appeared to dematerialize and was gone once again. I was too young to understand or realize it, but both my father and Houdini were philosophers.

Though I returned to my bed, I did not sleep again that night. I did not want to be a dreamer of the night. I wanted to be a dreamer of the day, dreaming my dreams with open eyes to make them possible. Isn't that what all of us really wish to do? And now I had been told as to how one makes that happen. I knew that whatever magic or special powers were imbued within me by my genetics, I also must apply myself arduously to my studies! In these evenings I was learning how much I was to be like my father and also learning how much I would be like Houdini.

***

It turned out that I was not the only one wandering the halls of our home in Glen Cairn at night or the wee hours of the morning.

Aside from myself and Houdini returning for a more careful review of the books in my father's study, others prowled about.

As it were, as the snakes Milo and Nigel had failed to retrieve Houdini's handcuffs, it was now Robert who had been sent to see about retrieving them for The Outer Circle's benefit.

The age of Glen Cairn meant that over the decades since its construction, its walls had been tunneled by a succession of vermin.

Moving from one place to another through the art of materialization was useful but it had its limitations and could not be used for certain purposes. Purloining the handcuffs through that art was not part of the possible. As such, Robert, in his vermin form, had become familiar with the various passageways through which rats could

scamper within the building. He was now quite cognizant of passages leading from the building's basement, up
through its walls, and then into our apartment. His night-
time plan was to sneak in as the rodent he was, morph
into his form as man-like, secure the cuffs from the study
shelf, and then audaciously leave with them through our
front door while we all slept.

The plan just might have worked save for a stroke of
luck that Houdini had chosen that very night to research
my dad's books.

When Robert transformed from rodent to man in the
library, Houdini had re-materialized in our home earlier,
checking some of the reference books my dad kept shelved
in the living room. Just as Robert was lifting the cuffs off
their shelf Houdini happened to return to the room and
found him there. Not prepared to tussle with Houdini
himself, Robert dropped the cuffs. Morphing back into his
rodent form, he rapidly escaped through a crevice where a
radiator pipe entered a wall.

The cuffs were an important link between the dimensions. Fearful that there would be future attempts to steal
them, Houdini made a mental note to alert my father.

CHAPTER 21

HOUDINI

IT WAS a fall of colder winds, winds that were supposed to bring an understanding of foreign ideas and fantastic new possibilities but also of winds that would bring untold evils.

It hadn't even been a week, yet how much the world had changed, or at least our perception of it. Houdini's return, in and of itself a phenomenal event, was now coupled with the specter of an evil organization with worldwide ties. Prior to this time, our world had seemed so much safer.

"I think I need to have a say here too," Houdini told me the next night. He wanted me to try to understand the theory and meaning of all that was in the notebook he had helped us to recover. His memory was returning and with it an understanding of his own past, present, and future; where he had been until now, how he had gotten there, and how he had returned. What he told me was difficult to follow and a bit confusing to me due to my age and his language being archaic or stilted, but I did understand clearly that he was no ghost and that somehow he had partially mastered an ability to transfer himself as energy to another plane and even to other times. This is how he tried to explain it:

"The mind and body are basically two different organisms. The body is given to the mind as a domain to rule over, control, and take care of. At birth the body assumes a prominent part in controlling the activities of the mind. The body wants its basic needs such as food, warmth, and comfort met. As the child grows older, the quality and strength of its personality is determined by the amount of authority that the mind can exercise over the body. The weak are those who have not the mental stamina to overcome the hold that their body has on their mind.

"Radio, television, and other means of communication between bodies now in vogue are purely mechanical, serving as means of communication between bodies, and individually between the minds which control or are controlled by these bodies. The time will come when the minds of all men will have learned to overcome the bonds of the body and will be able to communicate with others without any mechanical aid."

I was enthralled listening to the presentation of such thoughts, though I could not understand or completely follow everything he was telling me ...

"At present the body has considerable control over thought, particularly as to the activities of man, that is the carrying out of these functions such as to the obtaining of food or such. These functions occupy the minds of practically everyone. There are a few who spend their lives in thought such as philosophers, but these thinkers are merely occupied with the betterment of conditions for the body as a rule. The mind itself is seldom concerned.

"Man will learn eventually to distinguish between bodily needs and the necessity for advancement in the control of the mind. The mind learns its own potential.

"Therefore, it is the purpose of reasoning out man's existence that is the reason for its being. It will discover how to communicate with other minds. Thus, it will have reached its goal. When man's mind reaches this goal, there will be communication between the living and the dead as the decease of the body will have no effect on the mind. Items like the handcuffs that facilitated my return to the here and now and other portal facilitators will no longer be necessary.

"The body may be the battery of the mind but ultimately the mind will function on its own and find the energy necessary to exist without the body in this dimension, this time, as well as all the others.

I have begun to realize that one can exist on many planes and through many times, many places. Do you follow?" he asked.

"Clearly." I lied. There was just no way I could understand all of that kind of language. There he was, doing it again, talking to me as he had spoken to the three of us when he first "introduced" himself to David, Cheryl, and me the evening of Halloween. Too esoteric, I would describe it. I couldn't tell if he was serious about all of what he said. It did seem kind of far out, but what didn't as of late? I suppose it was a match for much of what had been found in his notebook but I must say that I was hoping for something a little more down-to-earth and easier for me to understand. And also, what *had* he been doing all of this time in addition to where *had* he been? Though he spoke of a returning memory, he left these questions unanswered and I felt perplexed. I really wanted to know him better and to have answers to these questions. Perhaps he noticed the expression on my face. I think noticing that, he began to describe more of what he had seen where he had been.

"You can hardly imagine what it is like as to where I was, the places I've been, the places I've seen. At times it was all so normal, but at other times, in another dimension it is marvelous. Have you ever used a diving mask?" he asked.

"Once," I answered.

He continued, "I remember how I used to look at the ocean and just see a sea of blue and was oblivious to what lay beneath. For so long the only world that existed was above water but when I began my underwater escapes, at first, since diving masks didn't exist, I put on some water-proofed motorcycle goggles to help me see what I was doing. It was then that I discovered a whole other world with creatures and plants and colors. What life is like for creatures of the ocean I could not have even imagined, Charlie. That transition, that difference, that is as close as I can describe it for you. It was the world of Jules Verne and *Twenty Thousand Leagues Under The Sea*. Well, part of it, where I've been is like that. Part is a whole other world, separate from the one we live in here.

"Unimaginable until there. And when there, you are perfect within it, as if you were a fish within the sea. Then this world, the one you and I are in now, seems foreign to you ... if or when you can remember it, for sometimes where you came from becomes lost as a memory until you are back there once again. Trying to describe that difference is just as unexplainable to another as the world we see when diving with a mask is so indescribable to someone who has never been diving. There you have it, as best as I can to tell you about what it's like to have been where I was."

Finally, this was a start in my really getting to know him. I guess, never having had any children himself, he had been talking to me as if I were an adult but then, stopping to notice my expression, he changed and began to relate to me in a manner more befitting my age.

Fortunately, clairvoyance was not part of Houdini's mastered talents or an acquired skill, learned or otherwise, so he couldn't hear my thoughts. Telepathy and clairvoyance are not exactly the same. But I *had* understood the gist of what he had said, and I think he now knew that was so. It was a beginning.

CHAPTER 22

OTHER TIMES?

- In the year 2505 Hereweald Weese became Extracorporeal Advisor Extraordinaire to the Central Consul of the World Federation Order. Scientific contributions attributed to Hereweald were responsible for the planet finally having limitless energy supplies due to advances in the use of heavy water and nuclear fusion reactions. Hereweald remains a somewhat reclusive figure. His early education, in fact anything about his early life, has remained a hidden factor and a mystery many have sought to learn of.

- In the year 1400 or so there is a story of a man or legend born of a virgin woman and incubus. Merlinus's life as a boy is not known, but as a man his powers as a soothsayer foretelling the lives of kings, of the rise and fall of great ramparts and their castles; of the walls protecting those who reigned within fighting to protect their associated lands, knowledge of those skills of Merlinus have been passed down through the centuries. Some say it is just legend. Some say it is history.

- Five hundred years prior to Merlinus, the onmyoji (one skilled in the way of the Yin and Yang), a man known as Abe no Semei appeared, or perhaps materialized, in Japan. That was somewhere around 950 CE. Like others seeming so similar throughout the centuries, his early history, his earlier life, remains obscure and the subject of various stories but no factual records can be found. It is hard to pinpoint his place of birth, to be sure of his parentage, or of any of his early childhood. Many villages have been happy to lay claim to his being from their particular province. A few descriptions of him have survived. They tell of a man of average height having hair that was jet black like most Japanese peoples, though somewhat curled. His eyes though were strikingly blue and curiously, otherwise, somewhat occidental in appearance. His talents or gifts for divining the unknown and predicting the sex of the unborn are legendary. Other tasks falling to him were those of protecting his city from bad spirits as well as providing explanations for poorly understood phenomena. His was a life that combined occultism with natural science. He made use of the Wu Xing, or the five elements, the source of the Seiman or pentagram symbol which came to influence Shinto, Buddhist, and Taoist practices; a symbol that began to appear in many places and on several continents.
- Though few know the story of another, one thousand or so years before Abe no Semei, around the time of the first century CE, there is a story of a man, a Jew, born in Bethlehem. Here too, that man's early days are somewhat obscure, his parentage also uncertain.

It is said he was born of a virgin birth. Little is known about his childhood but then, appearing as a man, he lived in Nazareth. Legend has it that in those days this miracle worker could turn water to wine and that he could heal with his touch. He had powers and skills otherwise unknown at such a time, perhaps taken from another time, another place.

CHAPTER 23

THE WEEKEND

FINALLY, FRIDAY morning came, and with it, an incredible sense of excitement knowing we were heading to Walter's in Maine. We arrived at school, got through the morning lessons somehow, and eagerly huddled together with David at lunch break talking animatedly in hushed voices about the trip.

Once home, Mother had everything packed and ready and standing next to the front door.

She was already back from her day of teaching as her students conveniently had early dismissal at times on Fridays. Father had taken the afternoon off and had just awakened from a nap. The drive to Maine was a long one and he preferred to have Mother keep us occupied rather than share the driving with him. The drive itself was around six hours. Since we would also be stopping for dinner and to get gas, it was likely to be after midnight by the time we arrived, hence pillows and blankets were near the door as well.

Father called for the garage to bring our gray Packard around and we began carrying everything to the elevator. By the time we got everything outside the building the car arrived. We quickly packed in, David included as his parents had left for Maine earlier in the day, and squeezed a bit to allow Mother to join us in the back seat as we were dropping the attendant off back at the garage. There, Mother moved up to the front seat and then off we were, up the Henry Hudson Parkway toward the New England Thruway and Maine.

We passed the time playing a game of who could spot the most out-of-state license plates. Mother kept track for us as you could only name a state once for it to count. We set a time limit of an hour for that. After Cheryl won that contest easily Mom began a sing-along, starting us off with a medley of familiar tunes that even Dad could join. While we were singing, I felt distracted and began to feel goosebumps popping up on my arms. Glancing toward Cheryl and David I noticed both were looking at their own arms.

Simultaneously I think we all knew that we were feeling "his" presence. Houdini was somehow here with us, in our thoughts, in our heads. Together we heard his voice, "Yes, I am here with you. I thought I might be helpful this weekend but think it wise to conserve my energy as much as possible. Getting myself from one location to another is just so much of a drain, so I decided to hitch a ride. My powers are also not strong enough to telepath your parents as well, it seems to take less energy to communicate with younger minds than with the more developed adult ones." Then there was silence again. Almost like he had dropped out of range. We were beginning to get used to the unexpected becoming an intermittent intrusion into what had otherwise been our normal lives, now becoming anything but normal and anything other than what was to be expected.

About half an hour later the discussion in the car turned to food and when the lights of a truck stop came up Father said, "Let's stop here and eat." Once the car was parked, we piled out toward the restaurant. While closing the car door my thoughts were interrupted by another voice in the ether saying, "Have a piece of cherry pie for me, it was always a favorite of mine and one of those mortal delights I have been missing."

Forgetting how my thoughts could be heard I thought to myself, "Really? Kind of a bit banal as a choice given how unusual everything else had been going."

To which, to my surprise, a response came, "Bess made the very best. I even got her one of those contraptions that removed the pits to make it easier for her. Once you all have this formula of mine figured out and I can perfect it, I look forward to regaining my full body again so that I can have the experience of eating some of my favorite foods!"

"Yummm," I heard in the ether around me, "cherry pie." With that, I knew what I would be ordering for dessert.

Once inside, a waitress called out to take any table we liked. We chose a booth since that was Cheryl and my favorite. We placed our order, milkshakes for David, Cheryl, and me along with cheeseburgers and fries. Of course, I asked if I could please have a piece of cherry pie for dessert.

"Cherry pie for Charlie?" Mom said.

"I'll explain my new taste later," I responded.

With that, David and I excused ourselves to the rest-room. "Did you hear Houdini asking me to order cherry pie?"

"I did," David answered, "and I wasn't sure at first whether he was talking to you or me. It's kind of hard knowing who is talking to whom when you're just hearing voices in your head." He laughed. While in the restroom we both saw a small rodent sitting in the far corner just watching us.

Looking in its direction David said, "Most unsettling, makes me unsure whether I'm still hungry."

"I know what you mean," I answered.

Back at the table David told everyone about our animal encounter.

"It was so strange," I said, "I actually had a feeling as if I knew the little fellow ... but not in a good way."

"Surely not," Dad said.

"Most unsavory," exclaimed my mother.

Cheryl remarked, "I hope there are not more of them in the kitchen where they're preparing our dinner."

"But let me tell you about our hitchhiker and why I ordered cherry pie ..." Then, in quiet voices, Cheryl, David, and I told Mom and Dad about Houdini's presence and his ability to talk to us in our heads, communicating in a telepathic fashion. They did not express surprise but rather nodded in understanding. Mom reached across the table to squeeze David's and my hand and Dad reached out for Cheryl's. Even without telepathy, close families and friends can understand what another feels. There are times when no words need to be spoken.

As expected, it was close to midnight when we arrived at the town of Gray where Walter and Litzka's house was in Maine. Even though it was late, the lights were still ablaze. Having napped the last portion of the trip Cheryl, David, and I were anxious to get inside and let everyone know about our "hitchhiker" and that there would be an additional unexpected house guest for the weekend ... one they wouldn't "mind" having.

The rest of the group had arrived well before us and there were empty plates with the remains of a cheese platter scattered about here and there. China Boy crowed his greeting as if it were already dawn. Settling in we joined those sitting around a large table in the main room and easily picked up in conversation where all had left off from the last weekend.

Walter brought us up to date with the fact that there still remained one totally enigmatic area of text: VIII.

The Gibson's home was exactly like I anticipated given Walter's occupation as a writer. Much like our own home, books were everywhere. They flowed like cataracts from the walls that were lined with bookshelves and spilled from there onto desks, tables, and even the floor. Walter gestured all around to them while saying, "I'm sure we can find something useful here or in one of the other rooms."

He and my father were clearly kindred spirits with respect to book collecting. At Walter's Maine home, Robert, his son, had covered every inch of wall space of the entire house with shelving for the books. Many of the shelves housed the pulp fiction stories Walter had written about The Shadow. Others were bending with the weight of copies of books he had ghostwritten for Houdini, Blackstone, or the Great Raymond. Walter could tell stories that went on for one, two, or three hours at times; stories about his backstage travels, filling our heads with the splendiferous illusions and tricks from the shows of an era now gone by. Some shelves contained a more select collection of texts, texts amassed through Walter's writing research and also gifts and additions from the oddest of places or most peculiar booksellers. And then there were a variety from magicians and even Houdini himself. Those were the books that had brought us to Maine.

Referring back to our uninvited guest Litzka said, "Hopefully Harry will point us in the right direction to help us see what is on those seemingly blank pages."

Unfortunately, since his comment about cherry pie, none of us had heard or seen him.

After we all were clear in saying so, Litzka added, "Then let's all get some sleep and approach VIII with fresh eyes after breakfast in the morning."

It really was quite late, or quite early depending upon how one viewed a particular day.

Once Litzka had shown us to our rooms for the night we all went off to sleep.

Not too many hours passed before there was a pecking at the door to the room where David and I slept through the little that was left of night. Looking toward where the annoying sound was coming from, I saw the door begin to open by an inch, followed by a peck and another inch of movement. From one or two feet off the ground, a brightly colored feathered head appeared. China Boy had come to rouse us from our slumber.

Having opened the door now open wide enough, he strode proudly forward before loudly crowing, being sure to wake our still sleepy heads, "Cock-a-doodle-do."

"And good morning to you too," I groaned before rolling over from my horizontal position and placing my pillow over my head.

"Cock-a-doodle-do," came again, this time just beside my bed and covered head.

"Enough," I said somewhat shrilly. And, not wanting China Boy to hop up next to me, I continued, "All right, all right all ready. I get the message. You want us up and working." David could not help but also now be awake and sitting up, looking dazzled, dazed, and also somewhat amazed to have a rooster in our room, as if that accurately described his expression. Figuring China Boy somehow understood our quest, we told him we'd get up and dressed but he should now go wake Cheryl next door. Seeming satisfied, and also understanding, he clucked once and then rushed back out the door turning his bantam tail feathers toward us and his head toward where Cheryl slept.

Once dressed we found Cheryl already down in the kitchen. Of course, our conversation turned quickly to wanting to know if any of us had heard from Houdini. As none of us had, Cheryl said that perhaps there were just too many adults about and that if we could be away from them then he might be more likely to appear or at least communicate. That sounded plausible. Knowing that the Gibsons also had a cabin down by nearby Lake Sebago, Cheryl suggested we check the barn for bikes. Finding several we opted for an early morning ride to the cabin.

There was only one road down to the lake so it was easy to find. Only upon arriving did it occur to us that maybe it was a bit unseemly for us to enter the cabin without the Gibsons being there. Reaching out tentatively and trying the handle I said, "Let's see if the door is open. If it is, surely then they wouldn't mind if someone went in, particularly if it is someone they know."

But it wasn't open. It was at that moment the three of us heard his voice. A voice once again in our heads, a voice that sounded like he had before, yet somehow also different. He began to materialize only to remain partially visible, then once again invisible. There was his voice though, his voice in our heads. "I don't know how to make that text visible, that text in the eighth section," he said. "You're right to come here. I want you to go inside and see if something can help with the answer. I gave many things to Walter, you know."

"But it's locked," David responded.

"No matter," he said, "You don't need to be a Houdini for this lock. I'll tell you where the key is hidden. Walter will never know. You need only take the key from under the rock by the backdoor step."

"Oh, I don't think that is a good idea," Cheryl said and both David and I shook our heads confirming that no, it was not a good idea at all.

Somewhat sternly a response came, "What's keeping you children from taking the key? Walter will never know that you have been inside unless you tell him. It's such chaos, papers and books all over the place. Seriously, he nor Litzka nor any of the others will ever notice. It will be our little secret. Wouldn't that be exciting?"

Then our heads seemed to lighten and our telepathic connection was gone. Cheryl immediately commented, "I don't know what both of you think but I do know that Mother and Daddy would certainly be ashamed of us if we followed Houdini's suggestion. I honestly can't understand why he would even make such a remark."

"It just didn't seem like the same person," I said.

"Really out of character," said David.

"Maybe we really don't know him at all, and I just thought we had a special connection."

Then David had another thought, "I don't think that was Houdini at all. I think there must be more than one person, thing, or entity that can communicate with us." Could that be? Like the adults, we had to keep that in mind.

Having said that we all somewhat gloomily returned to the Gibsons' main house wary more than ever of our perceptions.

After another day and a half passed without any further progress toward revealing the text of Section Eight, the text remained as it had been, an invisible enigmatic puzzle.

Somewhat disheartened and with no further contact from Houdini or a potential nemesis, the group decided to return to the city and follow up on the suggestion of Artie Shaw and Eleanor Roosevelt ... to visit the library crypt below the Cathedral of St. John the Divine.

CHAPTER 24

THE RODENT

ROBERT MATERIALIZED in the softly lit subterranean room where the occupants appeared to be virtually unchanged since he had last visited with them. His journey from Maine had been quick and he was barely queasy, a phenomenon that sometimes occurred when he shifted back to his human form to join his friends. He quickly surveyed the various groupings and his beady eyes settled on his favorites, his wife Ariel, and his mother, Limontina. Ariel was probably closer to Limontina in age but, of course, was still a very striking woman. Today she was wearing a clinging, long black slip dress that looked as if it was molded to her tall slim body. Her blood-red nails and lips matched Robert's red bow tie. When he could, he always wore a tuxedo. Usually it was a black one, but occasionally he donned a white jacket which made him look even more cadaver-like than ever. Ariel somehow seemed akin to a praying mantis in her movements. Limontina, in contrast to Ariel's black, was wearing a shapeless ivory chiffon dress with fringes reminiscent of the flapper style.

Perhaps she thought it would camouflage her corpulent physique, but the effect accentuated it. Milo Beard was seated with them.

Just as everyone else in the room, he had a pallor sported by those who never saw the natural sun. Robert twitched his mustache and raised his long hand, gesturing that he was back while expecting all to notice. Then he went to join Ariel and Limontina.

"I've got news, I've got news," he squeaked out. "You'll never guess who went along to Maine! What an unexpected treat!" With that he went silent, rubbing his hands together and occasionally touching his thin mustache.

Ariel turned to Milo and said, "Oh this is going to be so exciting, I'm sure. Why don't you fetch drinks for all of us to help Robert relax and share his story. I do so wish our old friends Adolf and Heinrich were here to participate in our undertaking. But then if we are successful in securing possession of Harry's notebook, we'll be able to bring them back to us again!"

"Of course, my lovely, *ssss*, and I will be sure to remember to give you two olives. Hitler is dearly missed, or were you referring to Eichmann in mentioning Adolf? You know, I've had good information from our friend Bishop Hudal that Eichmann is now in Argentina and will be contacting us soon. For myself, I look forward to having Himmler and Mengele back. What a joy they were! Just think of all the others who may soon be able to rejoin us. Yes, yes, what a joy it will be to work with them *alive* again."

Limontina couldn't help herself from adding in a few of her favorite friends now also gone. "Oh right," she exclaimed, "I've been reminiscing with Ariel about the times I used to have with King Leopold when visiting Belgium."

Milo was back in the blink of an eye, and Robert started his story.

***

While you may be wondering at this point why members of the Inner Circle didn't just materialize here or there at whim rather than using conventional means of travel, or why they might not just move objects without lifting a finger, I should point out that although the methods for such actions were available to the group, they were also cognizant of the limitations and ramifications of the use or misuse of such knowledge.

Some of the basic laws, when understood, make it quite clear that little good and potentially much harm could occur if the use of the techniques became rampant.

There was the concept of conservation of energy, that it was neither created nor destroyed. The first law of thermo-dynamics: In any process the total energy of the universe remains the same, but it could change form.

And then there was also Newton's third law of motion: To every action there is an equal and opposite reaction.

These premises should make it evident that if society in general started employing these techniques too freely, things would soon get out of control.

A simple analogy might be to imagine midtown Manhattan without stoplights. That would certainly have repercussions—or at the very least make it harder to get around.

So, when it came time next weekend for all to reassemble at the Cathedral of St. John the Divine and continue our analysis of Houdini's appearing blank Section VIII, those who were coming did not simply rematerialize at the appropriate spot. Instead, they took a more conventional means of transport: a car, a cab, bus, or subway, or they just walked.

That is not to say that no one ever used his or her special knowledge. It was more of a when, where, and why that should be answered first.

To those who were now part of the Outer Circle however, they often thought *and practiced* that any and all rules did not apply to them. So they did use the art, skill, and methods we all had learned too often and seldom for the right reasons.

CHAPTER 25

72 FEET UNDER
OR SUBTERRANEAN ARCHIVE

THE FOLLOWING weekend, late on Sunday afternoon, our group of decoders began to assemble at the Cathedral of St. John the Divine. Services had finished and we found Father McKeen in his vestry office.

Although the adults were familiar with the history of the subterranean archive, Father McKeen took the time to elaborate on the description he had begun for David, Cheryl, and me when we had first met while waiting for the group to re-assemble. He began to tell the group what he knew of the story of the *special* part of the cathedral's construction.

Leaning back in his chair and throwing open his arms, he said, "Big, colossal." His gestures were to allow for the great space the cathedral would assume, a space waiting to be filled with his descriptions. "That is the only way to describe the structure conceived by Horatio Potter—New York's Episcopal Bishop in the 1890s. Horatio died,

though, even before the first stone of this massive cathedral was placed. It was his nephew Henry who continued
the work, choosing architects and designs for the church.

"During Henry's watch, the 'trouble' with the foundation
became apparent—and with it the idea, practicality, and
appeal of a subterranean archive took on the reality that
some had hoped for and dreamed about. When the site was
originally chosen it was anticipated that it might provide a
unique location for a subterranean archive, but it was only
when they began to dig and dig did their dreams begin
to become fulfilled. The additional sums it was taking to
complete and to reach bedrock so far below ground would
have caused a normal project to cease right then. A new
location requiring less foundation work should have been
sought. Indeed, that is exactly what some suggested.
Building costs were out of control!

"It was then J. P. Morgan stepped in, offering half
a million dollars, a true fortune at the near turn of the
century, to finish the foundation work. It was a mystery
if not a folly to some—but not to those of the Inner Circle.
Seeing the possibilities of the great crypt beneath the
nave, Morgan was determined to ensure the creation of the
library. Others, not understanding the true significance of
the location, saw the location's problems as a detractor
from further construction. But Morgan continued to see it
as an attraction, and that led to his financial backing to
keep the project afloat."

Seeing that all stragglers coming from our home had
now arrived, McKeen stopped his history lesson and said,
"I will tell you the rest on the way down to the archive."
Standing up, he then motioned for all of us to follow him
while saying, "Come, follow me."

The church had many alcoves and artistic embellishments. McKeen led us to a side chamber through a small doorway from his office and then down a wide hall to a basement crypt where the Tiffany Chapel from the 1893 Columbian Exposition had once been installed. That area now had an unusual large painting behind a wrought iron protective fence. The painting appeared oddly dimensional and maze-like, much like a large Piranesi, with aspects that also likened it to the work of M.C. Escher. It was a picture of an Italian or Roman villa, but the dimensions were skewed to the imaginary, like Escher's later work, called "Belvedere." Unlocking a gate in the railing, McKeen walked up to the painting. Turning as if to walk towards the wall or a doorway of the scene, he then stepped forward and vanished, disappearing into the canvas.

Momentarily he appeared again and asked for us to join him. In reality, the painting was not flat but truly dimensional, creating an optical illusion concealing an entryway to the library below. Leaving the entry to the library open to view, it had actually been concealed, unguarded yet safe from those without proper knowledge. Much like the pickpocket looking toward the sky in Hieronymus Bosch's painting "The Conjurer," through optical illusion this work employed the art of misdirection. Though many in our group were well acquainted with this nifty deception, David, Cheryl, and I were amazed!

Litzka came over to join our group of three while at the same time nudging us forward, saying, "Come along, follow us." Then she too proceeded to vanish along the same path as Father McKeen. "Follow who?" I thought. Was she referring to herself and Father McKeen or herself and China Boy? As always, China Boy had come along in the carpetbag she carried at her side.

We quickly moved ahead, vanishing behind the painting to start our long descent at Litzka's and Father McKeen's heels. Much of the initial descent was through the above-ground structure of the church. The air coming from the passage was cooler, transformed by its ascent from the lower ground from where it had originated. Cheryl was quite reluctant to move into the space ahead since she was mildly claustrophobic and the staircase was narrow and dark, but the coolness of the air also reminded us again of Houdini. David went first, then I pushed Cheryl along, trailing behind her and then the others followed. Every four or five steps Cheryl would stop and I would have to give a little push to get her going again.

Seeing Cheryl's apprehension, McKeen took up where he left off, hoping his description would take her mind off the closeness of the walls.

"As you will soon see Cheryl, beneath the primary crypt at the cross of the church, the seventy-two feet required to reach bedrock eventually allowed construction of an enormous circular reading room several stories tall. Though the stairs are narrow at the start they will soon widen out, just follow me. You'll see that in no time we will be in a wider open area."

Sure enough, what he said was true, and in no time the smaller stairs had expanded, opening onto a wide-open stairway descending in a spiral fashion within a cavernous room. Father McKeen continued explaining as the group proceeded down:

"The outer perimeter of the room is lined by a series of arched galleries with reading areas along the balustrades and stack areas along the walls.

"Attached to the main reading room each level has one large entryway leading into additional two-storied stacks on the levels created beneath the nave. There is but a single set of stairs tracing a long spiral against the circle of the outer wall from its top to the bottom, broken only by a space for a landing at each level—of which there are five. The position of the start of the stairs at the side of the top main entryway lines up with the end of the stairs at the bottom level. The bottom level exists as a single room without an adjacent extension beneath the nave."

Cheryl was now thinking about his description and not the closeness of the walls, which had easily expanded to one yard and then more. She wondered how such a place could be built and remain a secret.

Sensing her thoughts, he ventured rhetorically, "How, indeed, was it built?" Then he proceeded to answer both his spoken statement and her thoughts.

"Construction of these areas proceeded in tandem with the general work being accomplished on the traditional foundation and crypt. You see, the cathedral was built by historic methods and style with solid carved and fitted pieces of stone—rather than with the newer available iron girders of the time—therefore few questioned the elaborate additional steps being taken on construction beneath ground level. An enormous cathedral naturally required an enormous and elaborate foundation. It was in this manner that building on the great archive remained a secret, even from those who were actually building it!

Only the engineers and architects, chosen from members of The Inner Circle, understood the complexity and truth of the plan. It would have been very difficult for the general construction workers to put two and two together as the steps needed to build the traditional foundation were incorporated into constructing the archive and vice versa."

It was clear that Father McKeen was very interested in the special space over which he was now the principal guardian. But his description, though elaborate, did leave at least me with another question which Cheryl knew that I was now thinking and she said out loud, "How did they get light into the area?"

"Ah, lighting such a large windowless space really wasn't a problem at all at the time. It was built during the transition period when the electric companies of Edison, Brush, and others were rapidly transforming all areas of the city and places from night to day. Gas lighting could have been used, but it was disappearing, giving way to the electric. It was decided however that some daylight would also be used in the space. To accomplish this, five lighting shafts were connected to the circular room within the columns supporting the balconies. Reaching up through the above-ground building of the church these structures began as skylights, capturing the daylight at the very top of the roof. Within the shafts, fittings were placed, aligning mirrors and lenses that intensified and reflected the light down to the lower levels whether the day was clear or overcast. Some of the light was directed to illuminate the parabolic ceiling over the main reading room, brightening it during the day while turning dark at night, but during the day focusing the best light to the lowest level on the ground below.

"You will see that near the base of each shaft, the light also filters down onto an opening designed as a position to place a text or document, a naturally lit reading stand or carrel, additional spaces for more detailed examination of material chosen for study. Had the newer electrical lamps proven to be unreliable, these were felt to be mandatory installations, while the conduits for the electrical wiring would have been retrofitted for gas.

"And a fact I find most interesting, one of the shafts had a further fitting with a piece of Iceland Spar—an integral part of a daylight timepiece we call Wheatstone's Clock using the principles of Charles Wheatstone and his observations of keeping time using polarized light. Unlike a sundial, this clock allowed the mechanism to function even on cloudy days." He mused for a moment and then added, shaking his head side to side as if dissatisfied with a portion of the construction, "The presence of that spar however does change the quality of the rest of the light that filters down to the reading carrel below and within that column. The light there is not as bright, making the space less suitable for functioning as a reading carrel."

Feeling like we were in another world, we continued our descent along the stairs and were offered glimpses down hushed corridors that led off from the different levels. The shelves holding the books were remarkable on their own—dark polished wood adorned with elaborate carvings. Some of the volumes they held appeared to be slowly moving, expanding in and out as if breathing the magic within. Others vibrated. A few glowed with a continuous, soft light while there were also those that blinked on and off with light. If not mistaken, I thought I heard sounds emanating from some of the pages. Passing the opening on one level there came murmurings as if the books were talking with one another. Here and there a book appeared to be floating, others were covered in frost. Odd bindings dripped and oozed or emitted smoke. Did I catch one winking at me? Perhaps beyond where I could see there were some with eyes and feet? There were darker corridors from which wafted a subtle hint of vanilla, decaying lignins—those complex organic polymers forming the basis of the structural materials from which paper and rags, but not parchment, were made. From other corridors came the smell of a mixture of spices, ancient roots, and barks combined with odors of herbs from long-forgotten leaves ... The only thing missing from our descent within the gothic stonework, I thought, were organ strains of Bach's "Toccata" and "Fugue in D Minor."

With a final turn we emerged from the dim light, finding ourselves at a large entryway atop a great space. The main archive Father McKeen had been telling us about was now before us, enormous and as he had described.

The circular, balconied walls were lined with bookcase after bookcase, each filled with leather-bound tomes both large and small, compilations of centuries of knowledge. Hundreds, thousands, perhaps tens of thousands there must have been. Although there were many reading tables, they were empty. We proceeded down the spiral staircase that lined the outer circular wall of the large chamber. Aside from what I believed were the murmurings of the books, level by level we passed the aged tomes and reading lamps, hearing only the echoes of our shoes as they traversed the many steps to the lowest level. As we circled lower, gazing across the vast space from one side to the other, a Wheatsone's clock came into view on the immense stone columns that rose from the floor to the domed ceiling.

As we descended past the last balcony to the final level, there was a lone individual seated at a central table, apparently awaiting our arrival. It was Houdini.

As we approached him, he stood up from the table and smiled at the group.

"Harry," McKeen greeted Houdini.

"You've aged," Houdini greeted him back, raising his eyebrows.

"Relativity has been good to you," McKeen said, now also smiling.

Walter, reaching for Houdini's hand, extended his own and when the two clasped Walter said, squeezing firmly and with a wink, "I'm so glad *all* of you is here," as Houdini now appeared fully corporal.

"Still the doubting Gibson I see, I always liked how you questioned things, Walter. But I may not be as whole as I appear to be," Houdini said with a concerned look overtaking his smile and then he said. "But the most important thing first. I fear there is little time to spare."

Turning to David, Cheryl, and me he said, "So you've brought them here with the book? And what do you think of the Eighth Section?"

Seeing him here, he seemed and sounded nothing like what we had heard when his words entered our heads as we stood outside Walter's cabin by the lake while up in Maine. Now his voice was warm and reassuring though with a hint of concern. He was much more like the person who spoke with me at night at home in Glen Cairn. Clearly the personage at Walter's cabin in the woods was not Houdini.

"Nothing," I said. "We've found nothing on those pages. We've tried everything we could think of on disappearing ink, but they're blank. We are not sure now that there is even anything on them."

Houdini answered authoritatively, "Well, there is. And I've brought you here to show you. The answer all of you and I myself have been looking for to elucidate my writings of the eighth form resides here in the cathedral. I finally remembered about the nature of the ink with which that section was written and how one could see the inscription." He looked over at McKeen and said, "You're aware of Wheatstone's clock and how it works but you've missed the potential of the difference in the grade of light it provides for the reading carrel. Those pages that appear so empty are covered in writings in ink made with Herapathite—polarizing crystals. The ink is invisible in regular light but when portions of the light that they reflect is canceled by another polarizing light, the cancellation will darken that area of the page, and the words become visible." While talking he had taken some of the sheets of his book and walked towards the reading carrel beneath Wheatsone's clock. As he placed the leaves under that particular illumination, writing appeared on the sheets, only to quickly vanish as he again withdrew them from the specialized light source.

"As many of you suspected, the methods I used to return are written here, but I have been learning and experiencing that they are incomplete and require refinement. And I am afraid that they may, well not just may but do in fact embody a fatal flaw.

"Many years ago, I met with Nikola Tesla as a member of our circle. As you know, he was a man of great genius, though often his genius was matched by great eccentricities, such as when he thought he was receiving communication signals from other planets. He was just beginning to unravel the methods by which I have returned, uncovering the first tenets of the process while working on his wireless transmission of electrical power. It was Tesla who sparked my continued interest and belief that such a feat was possible; to defeat death, to return to the living. He also helped resolve some of the formulative difficulties. Still there were formidable gaps in our knowledge. Dangerous flaws as it were.

"And Walter, remember Howard Lovecraft? H.P., we called him. You and he both wrote stories for that pulp fiction rag *Weird Tales*."

"Yes, I remember him," Walter said.

"You know, some of his tales and creatures were not totally fictional. We should talk about that sometime. Well, he worked with me when I was writing one of my books. He had a better education than I had which helped significantly in codifying my notebook. While working with him I had hopes at the time that he and I could start a college for the science of magic with courses formalizing and educating select students in the knowledge we have guarded so over the centuries."

"Really?" my dad said. "I wish I had thought of that. Perhaps it is something we should begin now, and with your help."

"Of course we should," Father McKeen quipped. "I can see it now with courses on the 'Philosophy of Magic,' the 'Psychology of Magic,' and the different disciplines of the 'Science of Magic.'"

"Yes, yes, but I'm digressing," Houdini continued. "Let me get back to why I've brought up Tesla ... these lofty intellectual ideas will have to wait a bit.

"Some of you know that I have been having problems maintaining form. But it is not just with the unusual materialization and reconstitution of life itself. The particular techniques I applied appear to have emphasized the dichotomy of my personality—indeed, I fear this method would with anyone's personality. It has caused an amplification of my good as well as my bad to a point of division, making it impossible to maintain a single individual form."

As we spoke, something unusual was beginning to happen to him. It was like there was a flicker of his image and he would appear slightly doubled, as two partially overlapped images, then single again, then doubled, and then taking shape as fully doubled. Standing before us now, there were two complete Houdinis! At that moment, neither spoke. They just looked at one another in a somewhat bemused manner, much in the same way we were also looking at them. Time seemed to stand still. No one moved.

Finally, after an indeterminate period of time, one of the Houdinis continued, "It is as I feared. The glue that forms us, the process of sublimation that checks our evil with good, can come undone."

Then the other Houdini answered, "Why fear when your better part can be freed? Don't you see what we have accomplished?"

I don't know what the others were thinking but I thought, "Will you look at this." And, of course, we all were staring at them. All of us were glued to our spots, aghast like little children coming undone, marveling at a fantastic scene occurring right in front of us.

Once again the other Houdini said, not to his other self but to us, "This has been happening for some time. It has taken all my power to pull together as one when it occurs, but it happens more frequently now. I had to have you bring the book here so that I can correct the formula, or if that cannot be done, then it must be destroyed."

Too overwhelmed by the proceedings we were witnessing, the group stood by motionless, watching and listening. Things were happening so quickly at this point that none of us could foresee the next events.

It took only one brief moment for the encrypted pages meant for possible destruction to be snatched from whom we perceived to be the "good" Houdini by the lightning-fast hands of the dichotomous "evil" twin. There was a brief glance by this thief in our direction, then the evil Houdini, raising his eyebrows, vanished.

The remaining Houdini looked at us again and said, "He will go to join the Outer Circle. That must not occur. *I* cannot let this happen." And with that, he too vanished. Poof, both were gone, leaving most of us with our mouths open, aghast as to what had just transpired.

At the same time an almost imperceptible motion caught my eye for I thought I saw a small rodent scurry along a side wall, slithering out of sight between the smallest of cracks.

Taking stock, the stakes had been raised. Never before had there been the possibility of bringing back not just the seemingly dead but also the dead in their most evil form— potentially an army from the dead to fill the ranks of the Outer Circle for new and unimaginable dastardly ends.

There was no time to spare. In the past, even the evil of those who found their way into Tte Outer Circle had been tempered by some good that exists in all of us, a good that may have been subjugated never to surface again, but somewhere a kernel did remain, a tiny element of good that, no doubt, kept at least something in check if not in balance.

With the ability to split evil totally and freely from good, the force and havoc that could follow might be beyond our comprehension. How could one fully understand, let alone deal with or overcome something never before seen? What would be the consequences of complete and unrestrained evil?

It wasn't a transmutation in that it wasn't one form transforming into another. It was a true splitting of forms. The good and the bad, totally separate. And never before had the world experienced what the force of unbridled bad could do. Bad that no human had ever portrayed. Far beyond the bad the world had known and endured under the reign of Caligula. Far beyond that suffered during the time of Genghis Kahn or the rule of Napoleon. Even beyond that of which our century's experience had been with Adolf Hitler. It was an evil that had previously been unknown but was now unleashed.

Like an epic tale, it was up to us, as a group, to try to retrieve the lost pages and restore the two Houdinis. That was the task before all of us. We had to put right something that should have never been, an unfathomable wrong—a lamentable mistake. And we would. We would gather all of the members of the Inner Circle. We would use the special powers learned over the centuries and we would plan and we would do battle. After all, there was not just an evil Houdini. There was also now one as the ultimate good. Two Houdinis, both unchained, having performed his greatest escapes; first from death and now from himself. Were the two equal? Was one more powerful?

Somehow, in this flash of a moment, in this parcel of time in a subterranean space, the world, as we had known it, had changed. The recent and immediate events, those eminent and those that were now likely to follow, the questions and all of the answers had transformed us. How much would life be like it was? Where would we fit into the world to come? We were no longer the children we had been. With only a memory of our young lives, a rapidly changing awareness of the present, and recently a glimpse into our future, we might not as yet have made the next leap to being fully adult but we had grown and had a better understanding of our place in the world and perhaps even the universe.

We did not know what the future held but knew we were to be an integral part of it and were now to take our places with others like ourselves in the world. Our outlooks had changed and broadened allowing us to persist and prevail.

We were ready for the task ahead.

EPILOGUE

WHAT MAYHEM occurred after the day at the cathedral, the day we all came together with Houdini! It seemed every week that no sooner than one bad deed had been accomplished then damage control had to follow.

How was our group to discuss the two Houdinis? At first it was a problem. Houdini 1 and Houdini 2 were too reminiscent of "Thing 1" and "Thing 2," the characters in *The Cat in the Hat* which had been published a year earlier. True, the Houdinis were in a sense similarly up to mischief, but not quite of the same kind and far from anything of such innocence. After a few suggestions were offered, we decided to simply refer to the good Houdini as "Houdini" and the bad one as "Harry."

There was, of course, also the problem of securing the handcuffs. We didn't want Harry to escape back into another dimension or another time to hide or live all the while being able to produce interminable harm and with only Houdini to chase after him. None of us has yet understood how the handcuffs worked or played into the ability of one to enter another dimension but they did, but that is another tale. We just didn't know at first whether harm could be done in those other dimensions or other times. We also were left with the problem of how to accomplish restoring the Houdini's as one, correcting his formula or helping him destroy it. This all had to play out, and play out it most certainly would.

Clearly, as the cuffs were a link to facilitate returning Houdini to where he had been or where he or, from now on, anyone might go dimensionally and through time, they had to be secured. Houdini's skill at opening locks and safes was legend, so their current location in our home safe and his knowledge that they were there meant that they were no longer secure. Sooner or later we were sure that the location of the cuffs and the portal they accessed would then also be known to Harry and become attractive to him to steal, use, and make his own. But where could they be hidden or sequestered? What location could possibly be impenetrable to our alter ego master magician and also out of sight and mind?

There is something else I can tell you now. The past is a sure place to be. It does not change. All those stories about someone traveling back in time and having to be careful so as not to change history? The butterfly effect? Hooey. Well, it just doesn't happen, so don't fret over that or spend any time imagining, "What if ..." Time happenings are fixed. What occurred, occurred. What will occur, will occur. Traveling through time will NOT change a thing. Though sure enough the Houdinis could travel in time, time is just not transmutable. No matter how one might try, one just cannot change how time unfolds, no matter the dimension. So, we will all apparently go through our paces and meet our fates. That does not mean there is no such thing as "free will." There is. The choices are ours, and those choices had better be smart ones. What was written is the result of those choices. What will be written is the choice we make as we make it. No one else can change it. That also does not mean that the events happening around us did not influence our choices. Confusingly clear now, yes? Essentially, when reappearing where one wasn't before, things occur to set the puzzle pieces back to where they would have been or always were and ultimately will be. That goes along with the science of actions and reactions, the conservation of energy. It even happens in the spooky science of particle physics. Go figure.

Soon I will sit down and write about the events that happened after the day our group reconvened and met up with Houdini in the subterranean library at the Cathedral. "What tales to tell," I mumbled a bit out loud.

"What is that you're saying," Houdini asked, looking up a bit tired from the desk where he sat as he so frequently did when writing out new formulas.

"Oh nothing," I answered. "Just thinking out loud on my own Holmes, um, I mean Houdini. Just scribing about our adventures past, present, and those still to come."

THE RELATIVELY SHORT REAL LIFE
OF HOUDINI AND THE REAL LIFE
OF THE YOUNGS, TRIPPS AND GIBSONS

THOUGH HOUDINI frequently would say that he was born in
Appleton, Wisconsin, what appears to be without dispute
today is that he was born in Budapest, Hungary. His name
at birth in 1874 was Erik Weisz, son to the Reverend Doctor
Mayer Samuel and Mayer's second wife Cecilia Steiner.
Including a half-brother from his father's first marriage,
there were four sons in the family. Whether Erik's father
was truly educated as a Reverend or had a degree designating him as "Doctor" is something of some dispute, but
that is not for this portion of our story to ascertain or
decide.

That said, Houdini's father was a learned man, and he
practiced as a rabbi, emigrating to America from Budapest
in 1876 at the age of forty-seven.

Just a few years later the complete family moved from
Appleton to Milwaukee when Mayer lost his post as rabbi
to the town's sole Jewish congregation.

Fortune did not smile on the Weisses once in Milwaukee
and young Erik helped family finances through multiple

odd jobs. During that time Erik developed an interest in secular pursuits mainly as an entertainer, at times a trapeze artist, and also by performing acts of contortion.

As steady work continued to elude Rabbi Mayer in Milwaukee, once again the family picked up and moved, this time to New York. Unfortunately, steady work as a rabbi remained just as elusive there so, ultimately, he took steady work along with his son Erik at a Broadway neckwear-cutting firm.

Education for Erik appears to have been slim but did include becoming a pupil of Zichon Ephraim in the Talmud Torah.

Perhaps the first significant appearance of Erik as Houdini occurred after he and his friend Jacob Hyman teamed up as the "Brothers Houdini" sometime around 1891. The "Brothers Houdini" was a magic act. Erik's initial interest in magic appears to have been fostered after receiving a box of magic tricks when he was a child in Milwaukee.

His taking the name Harry Houdini is likely due to two things. Erik's nickname was "Ehrie." Anglicizing Ehrie phonetically became Harry. The name Houdini was Erik's tip of the hat to the father of modern magic, the French conjurer named Eugene Robert-Houdin. Many magicians of the era would also add an "i" to the end of their names, likely because of the prominence and memory of a great Italian conjurer from the 1700s called Pinetti.

Jacob Hyman left the team of two in 1894 and Harry's brother Joe briefly became the second brother of the act. Shortly after, Joe was replaced by brother Theodore. Theodore later took the stage name "Hardeen" and continued to perform magic throughout his career, often performing similar illusions and escapes as those performed by his ultimately more famous brother. Their act was the first to include what became one of his staple illusions, the trunk transformation called Metamorphosis.

The Brothers Houdini ended later in 1894 shortly after Harry had met Wilhemina Beatrice Rahner. Beatrice soon became his wife whom he came to call Bess.

For several years Houdini and Bess traveled about as five-and-dime or variety show entertainers, often barely making ends meet. Their signature act was the performance of the trunk trick Metamorphosis. Metamorphosis was developed from a similar effect performed in America by the Davenport brothers and one performed by J.N. Maskelyne in England in the mid-1800s. The trick involved Harry being restrained, bound up in a sack, and locked into a trunk. Bess would then close a curtain hiding the trunk. After a few moments, she would step behind the drawn curtain. Nearly instantaneously Harry would step out from behind the curtain, unbound. He would then open the curtain revealing the locked trunk. Unlocking and opening the trunk he would help a figure stand up from within the trunk, a figure enclosed in a sack. Opening the sack revealed Bess, fully shackled or bound. Metamorphosis.

Even with this trick, fortune did not shine on the couple. Near the time that failure as entertainers seemed clear, the showbusiness break that had eluded them finally came.

While performing in St. Paul, Minnesota, the famed vaudeville entrepreneur Martin Beck saw Houdini perform. After Houdini successfully escaped from hand-cuffs, Beck had brought to test him, Beck offered Houdini a contract. From that contact, a star was born! Houdini went on to become famous for performing magic and escape acts not only throughout the United States but also throughout much of the world.

Early in his career, Houdini developed an interest in spiritualism. First this appears due to its association with tricksters or fraudsters and the use of its effects for show business and carnivals.

Later in life, he used his skills and knowledge of sleight-of-hand and the performance of illusions in an effort to debunk the performance of the spiritualists of his day. Through his personal correspondence and other writings, it is clear that although he might have liked to believe in an afterlife, he remained forever a skeptic. In a letter to Upton Sinclair dated June 10, 1924, he wrote, "You understand I am not an enemy of spiritualism. [sic] Am seeking the truth, but my years of experience in mystifying investigators allows me to look in the gloom of mystery where the great majority have to grope in the darkness. The scientist is not qualified to catch pickpocket or a crook."

Houdini's death on Halloween in 1926 came as the result of peritonitis secondary to a ruptured appendix. Though this occurred in close association with an unexpected blow he sustained to his abdomen a few days prior, the blow is unlikely to have been the direct cause of the rupture. He was operated on for appendicitis at Grace Hospital in Detroit. It was during his post-operative period in the few days before his death that during one of Bess's visits, she related that he told her, "Be prepared, if anything happens." Bess took that to imply that she should not only be prepared for his possibly imminent death but also that she should keep in mind the compact they had made that when he died, he would try to reach her from the other side, the side after death. That pact resulted in the yearly séances she would hold for a complete decade after his passing, séances held on the anniversary of his death, on Halloween. After that time, it fell on those close to Houdini, such as his intermittent ghostwriter and amanuensis Walter Gibson, to continue the tradition. In fact, she approved and asked Walter directly to carry on the tradition after she decided that the continued effort would be futile.

Walter went on himself to become famous as the writer of *The Shadow* novels under the pen name Maxwell Grant.

As to how the Youngs fit into the story ... Yes, the Youngs were and are a real family.

Morris Young was born in Lawrence, Massachusetts in 1909. Early in life, he developed an interest in "things magical" and held magic shows entertaining school friends with his younger brother Barnard. Around the time he was a student at MIT, Morris developed a cataleptic levitation act which he was able to demonstrate to Houdini during a publicity visit Houdini made to the Lawrence/Boston region.

Later in life Morris, along with his wife Chesley Barnes, became a magic collector and together with John McManus and John's wife Hanna amassed one of the great libraries on magic. In 1955, they donated their combined collection of over 17,000 books and related materials on magic to the Library of Congress. The gift augmented Harry Houdini's books and papers that were already a part of the library's permanent collection. At that time Morris was practicing as an ophthalmologist in New York City. His wife Chesley had an early career as a cryptologist while serving as a Captain in the Women's Army Corps in World War II. At times she had been on loan to the British forces. Morris was inducted as a member of the Inner Circle of the Magic Circle of London, England.

Through associations made during World War II, as well as through Morris's brother Barnard, who was active as a music publisher, they developed an eclectic group of friends and acquaintances. Many of that group have parts in this historical fiction. Of note in this tale are Eleanor Roosevelt, Eartha Kitt, Orson Welles, Artie Shaw, Umberto Eco, Harry Blackstone Sr, Eli Wallach, and Walter and Litzka Gibson.

The children, Charlie, Cheryl, and David, are real too, though lacking any "special powers" other than what could come through good schooling. The United Nations International School played a part in their early education.

During the 1950s both families, the Youngs and the Tripps, lived on Riverside Drive in Manhattan in a building named Glen Cairn. Paul Tripp created *Tubby the Tuba* as well as hosting several nationally televised shows including *Mr. I. Magination*, *On The Carousel*, and *Birthday House*. He was a headliner in the perennial movie *The Christmas That Almost Wasn't*. Ertha Kitt lived in the penthouse. The building and its apartments were, and to a fair degree still are, much as described.

Walter and his wife Litzka were frequent visitors to the family home. Walter and Morris wrote a few books together. Some of their books include *Houdini's Fabulous Magic, How to Develop an Exceptional Memory, and Houdini On Magic.* Litzka did indeed have a pet rooster she had named China Boy and she always brought China Boy along when they came for dinner. More than once she told the children's fortunes and would sit reading their palms. China Boy, having a language of his own, made intermittent comments during their times together though some would call them "clucks."

Visits to places like the Grill Room at the Hotel Taft were regular weekend occurrences. There, hours would pass for the children sipping Shirley Temples and Roy Rogers. The adults listened to music played by Vincent Lopez's Orchestra and, if not playing with the orchestra, at times conversing with Artie Shaw. Morris's brother Barnard was one of Artie's and Vincent's music publishers. All were family friends.

As to the evil "Outer Circle," several people and even one or two organizations provided inspiration for developing those characters. Saying more about just who those individuals or groups might be would be inappropriate. Suffice it to say though that none of those folks are still alive to guess if they are the ones described and none of the groups currently exist.

Growing up as we did at Glen Cairn, having the interactions with writers, actors, magicians, performers, philosophers, intellectuals, and people of note, it wasn't difficult to drift from reality and wonder at times "what if" or "what IS real." Our life was a story being written as we lived it, making it easy for us to write this particular historical fiction. To this day both Cheryl and I can find ourselves wondering what was or perhaps was not real, and having to stop and think, "am I remembering, or am I making this up," while writing and that, I suppose, is why it is historical fiction and not just fiction, and why it can be difficult to know the difference.

Some stories are just stories. Others are more. You'll have to decide about this one.

ACKNOWLEDGEMENTS

As most authors will tell you, writing a novel is a process, particularly, no doubt, when it is your first. So much has to happen after having that first idea. For us, there were many stops and starts in the writing process itself before a publisher was found. And then the real work begins.

The first draft of *Houdini's Last Handcuffs* was sent to my eleventh-grade English teacher, Daniel Menaker. At that point in time, in 2004, the book was titled *Growing Up With Houdini*. Mr. Menaker had already written a novel of his own. He had also become editor-in-chief at Random House so I figured his guidance could be helpful.

Indicating that I had been his former high school English student in my approach letter, Mr. Menaker was kind enough to respond with a handwritten note offering what I would call constructive criticism. To me, that was encouraging and I thought, OK, I'll rework the writing with his comments in mind. Then I set the work aside waiting for further inspiration to strike.

My main work as a physician and raising my family took over and somehow the years slipped by before I reached for the manuscript again. Ever so slowly, I began rewriting the book. Showing it to my sister, given the subject matter involved our combined upbringing, she took an interest which led to her contributing chapters. Eventually, in 2021, our completed work was submitted to Vine Leaves Press. We are appreciative that they were interested in having us publish with them. With that in mind, we thank both Jessica Bell, our publisher (who also created the cover art for this book), and Amie McCracken for having confidence in the work.

Additionally, we thank our editor, Melissa Slayton, without whom our work would be much less than it is now.

We gratefully acknowledge the inspiration of our parents, Morris and Chesley Young as well as Walter and Litzka Gibson, who surrounded us with a loving, creative, and imaginative environment that helped foster the creation of this story.

Other individuals without whom this work would not have reached completion include David Tripp, Diana Pollin, Georgiana Groen, Alan Kurzweil, Joseph Caldwell, and Douglas Martin.

We also thank the International Brotherhood of Magicians for permission to reprint the article written by Morris N. Young, M.D., "The Last Handcuffs."

THE LAST HANDCUFFS

BY MORRIS N. YOUNG, M.D.

Reprinted with permission from The International
Brotherhood of Magicians, *The Linking Ring* 1992

Accompanied by Hardeen's widow, John McManus and
I stepped down into the cellar of her home at 537 East
21st Street, Flatbush, in Brooklyn. We were respectfully
curious.

Confronting us was a dismal scene that resembled the
litter inside an abandoned barn. There was a shambles
of wood, metal, cloth, paper, boxes, trunks, and otherwise
not readily identifiable objects. Hardeen had been gone
almost six years.

Permission was given to John and me to take whatever
we wished, but to have the place cleaned out by the end
of the week, as Mrs. Elsie Hardeen was moving out. She
related that since her husband had passed away, many
people had scoured the cellar, purchasing or taking whatever they liked. Al Flosso was the last to do so.

John, an attorney, chose to stand by, chatting with Mrs. Hardeen about legal problems which had been concerning her. While they talked, I began my tour of inspection for finds. A quick survey noted that the central open area of the basement was bordered by a coal bin, an open alcove, and a small storage room. The fourth wall was covered with aging brown boards.

A body-shaped framework made of wires lured me to the alcove where it lay upon a heap of crumbled dirty tarpaulin-like cloth. No other parts for an Astra illusion were locatable thereabouts. The next attraction was the coal bin from which a frame of metal with mahogany colored sidings peeked out. Two more similar contraptions were stacked in the open bin, each frame enclosing different designed slats, and all recalling a top for the Chinese Water Torture Cell. Mrs. Hardeen explained that "They" had been working on various types of improvements.

Quite heavy and large, the tops would have required a larger vehicle than we had for transport. Reluctantly, we abandoned them.

Turning to the storage room, I was greeted by stacks of brown paper wrapped packages, some of which had been opened and contents strewn around. There were copper cuts, leaflets, and mats, all of which pertained to Houdini's film projects, serving as promotional material. In a corner were bundles of the "Margery" exposure booklets, and pamphlets titled, *Life and History of Hardeen*. After selecting a few of each item for John and myself, I reentered the large central open area of the cellar.

I was transfixed by a lobby display board from which Houdini's face regarded me intensely. The painting had become grimy with time. Another large lobby display board, painted black, from which many cut wires protruded, still had a small metal plaque attached, with barely legible words referring to a jail lock that had once been affixed above it. I removed the plaque (which is now to be seen at the Houdini Historical Center).

A sweeping glance identified several metal trunks and a wooden box of drawers, next to be examined. There was much rubble everywhere that had to be stepped on or over, such as carpenters', plumbers', and electricians' tools and supplies, a treasure trove for maintaining a house. Two of the large trunks were empty, not prepared in any way to use in illusions except for storing or shipping purposes. The third trunk, with "Houdini 8" painted on it, demanded investigation.

Many of the items in this precious trunk and the box of drawers standing alongside are described by me in the December 1951 issue of MUM. They are the basis of an exhibit at the Houdini Historical Center. Trunk 8 yielded a book on mechanical movements and another on the steel square, that was autographed by J. Collins, Houdini's valued assistant. Separately tucked away in one of the adjacent box drawers, the inventory book of Houdini's successive shows was discovered. John and I gave all three books to the Library of Congress.

We proceeded to gather together many small objects and pack as much as possible into John's car, to be checked through as to those we felt warranted retention for historical preservation. Then Mrs. Hardeen invited us to her late husband's bedroom where we might be tempted by other memorabilia.

Captivated by the aura of the room, I was fascinated by a small round mirror on a stand, perched on the dresser, that seemed out of place. Mrs. Hardeen explained that it had been her husband's make-up mirror, which always accompanied him on tour.

Nearby, a tray of trinkets contained several gold-plated buttons on which the letter "H" was fashioned. They were from jackets worn by Hardeen and members of the show.

John took the mirror and I picked up two of the buttons, one of which is now at the Houdini Historical Center. The mirror joined Ken Klosterman's Salon de Magie.

Before leaving the house, I returned to the cellar for a final look, hesitant to depart because of the almost supernatural spoor of the brothers Houdini and Hardeen that lingered. A glint from an opposite wooden wall led me to become aware of a somewhat dusky pair of handcuffs fastened to it just above eye level by bent nails. It may never be known why Hardeen had placed it there, or never disposed of it, or why not one of the dealers, friends or collectors had latched on to it. Perhaps, like a horseshoe, the handcuffs had been nailed up "for Luck."

Mrs. Hardeen assured me that there were no other restraint devices in the house aside from the torture cell tops. She did have a small bag of picks treasured by Hardeen and Houdini, but had been instructed never to give them to anyone. They were to be kept in a vault or destroyed. Without demonstration of any emotion, she gave me permission to detach and keep the handcuffs.

Within two days, a friend I contacted removed all tools and debris from the cellar. Eagerly, another friend picked up a set of narrow tail mirrors, the remains of an illusion, to use them for decorative purposes in his Great Neck, Long Island, home.

Hauntingly, the instructions Houdini had recorded in his last will and testament shouted through my mind ..." devise and bequeath to my brother Theodore Franz Weiss, professionally known as Hardeen, all my lithographs, theatrical effects, new mysteries, and illusions and accompanying paraphernalia to be burned and destroyed upon his death ..." Recalling this, I sought to reconcile reality with dashed hopes.

Possibly, Houdini had taken a cue from Hofzinser, an Austrian magician genius of the early 1800s, who had wanted to have all his magic properties done away with after his death. Apparently, Mrs. Hofzinser did not comply. Perhaps, too, Houdini's instructions, if revealed during his own lifetime, would add to the luster of the Houdini fable. It could also serve as a footing for Hardeen, in establishing him as successor for presentations of the deceased mystericist's show.

It may be that economic pressures played an insidious role in directing Hardeen's course of action. He sold off most of the important materials, allowing little for his wife to dispose of similarly. After John McManus' and my final screenings and what our kind friends carted away, the customary agencies of civic sanitation were called upon for the final dispersal, except for that "little bag of picks."

Moreover, that tantalizing pair of handcuffs which I had removed from a cellar wall was the last representative handcuff to be released from the Houdini-Hardeen estates and escape oblivion. From a collector's point of view, what a prize!

Houdini in his writings had identified its type as a Tower and Lyon Double Lock. He described a special pick for opening the cuffs. The cellar pair differed as to the linking chain. Instead, each cuff had smaller links with longer chain strands, clasp ended, that could be interlocked readily. One of the cuffs was provided with an almost undetectable gimmick for opening, not needing the clumsier pick that had been publicized in exposures.

For years, the vague implications of the find, and the circumstances surrounding that occasion continued to vex me. The challenge reinforced my determination not to sell, trade or give it up, although many collectors and others tendered tempting offers.

One day I received a letter from the newly inaugurated Houdini Historical Center. The ingenious use of a handcuff to join together the letters "O U" in Houdini's name as depicted in the letterhead startled me. I rushed to compare it with my handcuff relic. Both cuffs were identical in shape.

There is no clear explanation as to what may have impelled the designer to create the iconographic likeness. The last pair of handcuffs from the Hardeen home had called attention to itself in the true Houdini tradition.

VINE LEAVES PRESS

Enjoyed this book?
Go to *vineleavespress.com* to find more.
Subscribe to our newsletter: